MEANWHILE
ON
A ROOF
IN
CHINATOWN

Triangle Ranch Worldwide is an imprint of Triangle Ranch Communications.
Triangle Ranch Communications
526 N. West Ave. #43
Arlington, WA 98223
www.triangleranch.com

Originally published in Swedish by Isaberg förlag in 2011. The English version published with permission by Isaberg förlag
www.Isaberg.nu

Cover design by Johan Vipper

Ordering information:
Quantity sales. Special discounts are available on quantity purchases by organizations, associations, and others. For details, contact the publisher at the address above.
ISBN: 978-0-9885519-2-3
First American Edition

MEANWHILE ON A ROOF IN CHINATOWN

a novel

Ingrid Rudefors

translated from the Swedish by Odella Schattin

Triangle Ranch Worldwide

*Once upon a time, before cell phones and coffee chains
spun their web over the world
When the towers still stood tall—*

Prologue

In a kitchen in Äppelviken near Stockholm, an elegant middle-aged woman is having a nervous breakdown. She can't stop shaking and has to sit down for a while. She's not about to faint. Not at all. The floor has simply disappeared beneath her. When the phone rings, she spins around and accidentally knocks over a glass pitcher, sending it crashing to the floor. She leans against the kitchen counter and slowly sinks down into a sitting position amid the shattered glass. Weeps silently. Picks up neither the phone nor the broken glass.

When the phone stops ringing, the woman gets up and leaves the kitchen. Her breakfast remains uneaten on the counter. Shards of glass are strewn all over the beautiful mosaic floor. She plods her way forward as if through thick snow.

Then she leaves. Suitcase in hand. The elegant, middle-aged woman, named Alice, closes the door behind her, not bothering to lock it.

* * *

At the same time, on the roof of a tenement building on Catherine Street in New York, a skinny young woman, her reddish-blond hair in a tight ponytail, is enjoying the last sip of a Brooklyn Lager. The beer has a floral taste, mild. Not the least bit aggressive and crisp.

This is her second beer in the half hour she's been on the roof and it slips down smoothly.

The building is in lower Manhattan, tucked away behind the scenes of tourist-Chinatown. Across the street is a factory building, with its dirty brown brick facade. On the third floor, women are toiling at sewing machines in an illegal sweatshop without unions, social security or lunch breaks. They just sew. On the floor below them, a middle-aged Asian couple is arguing by an open window. Their voices carry into the street and hit the wall of our girl's building. A group of men is practicing tai chi in the room next door to the arguing couple, their movements graceful, a cross between poetry and violence.

The girl is watching the street below where a couple of shop signs in Yiddish are testament to other immigrant groups that dominated the area in the past. The scent of Chinese herbs blends with exhaust fumes and the stench from puddles that are cultivating their very own bacterial universes. Green shimmering puddles that you'd rather not step in. Especially if you're wearing scanty summer sandals without socks, which, of course, you are. The heat lingers on although it's well into September.

The view empowers the girl—the excessive inhumanity hasn't hit her yet. She drinks to build up courage. Soon Gabor will be home and the complications will begin. She knows it. She stands there, the empty beer bottle in her hand, regretting that she didn't bring up one more. The two beers have made her tipsy. Three would have made what she has to say much clearer, more definite. Alcohol has a way of making thoughts so comfortably reasonable. But the beer is gone and soon she'll have to go downstairs. She wants to try to explain things that she doesn't really understand herself; how can you know that you love a person if you are still with him? She has an uncomfortable feeling that love is something you discover when it's too late—so why not try out a variety of lovers in the meanwhile? After all, she's only twenty-five, with beautiful breasts and a mouth that loves to be kissed. There's still time. Even though time no longer seems as endless as it did when she was twenty-three.

* * *

Alice doesn't know how she got here. She is standing at the Scandinavian Airlines counter staring at the man in front of her.

A swarm of bees in her head.

Heart beating arrhythmically.

Obsessed with getting to the front.

Looks neither left nor right.

Nor behind her.

Is just here.

Now.

The ticket agent is tearing a piece of paper, v e r y slowly.

New York," she says out loud, urgently. At least she thinks she does.

Is she saying it out loud?

He doesn't look up. It's as if she's not there, as if her voice doesn't carry. But she has no time to be polite.

"The next plane!" She is almost screaming.

The ticket agent looks up in surprise. Calmly. Leisurely. Adjusts his glasses. It takes forever before he asks, "Reservation?"

She shakes her head. Doesn't he get it?

"It'll be pretty expensive," he says, still so aggressively calm and solicitous. "People usually book in advance."

Alice takes out her gold card and throws it down on the counter, looking away while he processes the ticket. Everything he does goes in slow motion.

She takes the ticket and doesn't bother checking the price—at this point, what difference would it make?

She checks in.

Goes through security.

She sits down on a hard plastic bench. And finally, the tears start to flow. Her whole body is shaking, out of control. She can see how people hurrying by on their way to the duty free shops glance at her in fright.

Inside Alice there is a black bottomless pit dragging her down, down. But she collects herself—gets up, walks over to a bar and orders a Jameson. A double.

* * *

Catherine Street lies east of the Bowery. To the west is tourist-Chinatown. So near, and yet a completely different world. Everything there is legitimized with English translations on the menus. But if you know where to look, you can still find illegal fireworks, smelly medicinal concoctions and other exotic secrets behind the counters of the local souvenir shops. In contrast, on Catherine Street you won't get very far at all unless you're fluent in Chinese. And if you're not Asian by appearance you may well have to wait a long time to be served at the local grocery store.

The smell of slightly rotten Chinese vegetables permeates the air. The crowds are gone. Chinese shop owners and restaurant customers alike are on their way home to the larger Chinese neighborhood in Queens, leaving only large mounds of garbage behind them. The street is illuminated by a sole pink neon sign on the corner. **B A R**, it simply says.

This bar is not part of the local Chinese influx, but rather a remnant of the old Bowery, where bars are simply bars, where the sole purpose is to drink alcohol. Nothing else.

From her vantage point on the roof, the girl with the beer watches as the woman who works at the bar called BAR unlocks the door and disappears into obscurity. The girl doesn't know her. She has never set foot in the bar which is mostly frequented by two, three depressed figures who, she imagines, smell bad. She's never given much thought to why that beautiful dark-haired woman chooses to work there. She doesn't really fit in, but then again, no one fits in anywhere in New York.

Maybe that's why she likes living here. The only thing that has ever been remarkable about her is her name. In what must have been a spurt of pretentious insanity, her mother named her Babylonia. A mammoth name she knows she will never grow into. Her friends call her Babs, for short. And even that doesn't fit. She is neither a heavy Babylonia nor an easy-going Babs. She's more of an ordinary Lena.

A van with Chinese lettering speeds by, headed towards the East River. Some kittens eat from the garbage under a closed vegetable stall. In the distance, a tall Hungarian guy comes walking down the street. It's Gabor, wheeling his bike. The girl waves but Gabor can't see her where she's sitting on the roof. She tilts the bottle, sucks down the last drops of beer and trudges down the stairs dreading the serious talk that awaits them.

But Gabor has rented a movie and brought home a six-pack of Heineken. Babylonia falls asleep in front of the TV. Slightly drunk. Unfortunately. The talk never happens.

* * *

Across the Atlantic, a middle-aged man walks into the villa in

Äppelviken. He's in a hurry, stopped home just to pack a few things before his flight to a conference in Berlin. His scalp itches. He should take a shower but doesn't have the time. It'll have to wait until he gets there. He considers a shot of whiskey to unwind. Goes through the mail, takes off his shirt, picks up a glass and bottle—and stops short. Starts walking around the house uncertainly.

He tiptoes gently over the glass shards on the floor, picking up the remains of breakfast from the counter. The butter has melted. He opens the dishwasher and discovers all the wet neckties. He stands there for a long time just looking at them. A shimmering green, soaking wet tie in his hand. Slowly, cautiously, he goes upstairs. Wary of the confrontation he expects. Realizes, however, that it's inevitable.

But in the bedroom, on the empty bed, he finds only a note. He picks it up, reads it and looks around. Slowly, he makes his way to the window. He looks out over a vista of private homes. The leaves have begun turning. Children wearing rain gear are playing in a neighbor's yard.

Two cars are parked in the driveway. One small and one large. He leans his cheek against the glass, the note in his hand.

* * *

The cramped apartment on Catherine Street houses two other residents. One is a beautiful panther-like cat named Elvis and the other a corpulent gray-striped tabby named Loser.

They hate each other.

While Gabor and Babylonia sleep, Loser, the fat cat, pins Elvis down to the floor. He has his teeth on the other cat's slender neck. Elvis lies still until a large cockroach scurrying across the floor captures Loser's attention and Elvis is released.

* * *

Alice stares down at the laminated card that carefully describes how she can save herself.

Take off your shoes.

Put your head between your knees.

Put on an oxygen mask and breathe normally.

Find the nearest emergency exit.

An emergency exit? How can this laminated "in case of catastrophe" plan possibly help her?

She wants to get off.

Change her mind.

But the plane has taken off—and now it's too late.

1

From April through October, the windows at each end of the apartment stood wide open. Sounds bounced through the rooms; noise from goods being unloaded, voices shouting at one another, cars honking insistently. A cacophony, like a concert in which it is quite impossible to distinguish individual instruments. Coughing car motors refusing to start, subway trains rattling and creaking in the underground, someone laughing, maybe someone swearing at a broken shoelace. The sounds of sex from thousands of people having intercourse before they hurry off to their jobs, coupled with the sound of someone grinding coffee. A few hundred people singing in the shower, heels clacking on the asphalt, police and fire truck sirens mixed with the voices of four angry workers who discovered a car blocking their access to a manhole.

Babylonia was often awakened by trucks that sounded as if they were idling inside the apartment. With her eyes closed, she pretended that her bed was in an outdoor market. That she lived on the street and not at the top of a six-story apartment building on Catherine Street.

Gabor lay naked beside her, asleep on his stomach with his mouth open. He was hairy all over. Even on his back.

Rózsadomb—Äppelviken. The same background. Yet so different. She watched him quietly, not wanting to wake him, just letting her finger lightly touch his shoulder where black hair grew like thin grass. Enjoyed the safe solitude of lying awake next to someone who's sleeping. He looked relaxed and calm as he slept, completely different from when he was awake—her Gabor, Eeyore the donkey with a black cloud of melancholy hanging over him wherever he went. A heavy locomotive that she had to push with all her might if they were to get anywhere at all. He loved mournful Eastern European classical music and arcane intellectual jazz. It was completely incomprehensible to him that you might listen to cheerful soul or hip-hop while doing the dishes just because the music gave you energy and made you happy.

If you read, you had to do it seriously.

When you listened to music, you had to sit quietly and concentrate.

God, she was so tired of him!

* * *

Alice wrapped the blue airplane blanket around her. Disliked the proximity of the man in the seat beside her. He was watching a movie and was on his third whiskey. She had just finished a second glass of wine, preceded by a Bloody Mary. She couldn't even remember the last time she'd had a Bloody Mary.

She leaned her head against the window, as far away from the man as she could, closing her eyes. Noticed that the alcohol was going to her head, but right then it felt quite pleasant.

What had she done? Oh my God, she hadn't even called work. Could it be that she'd been crazy for a long time now and had simply managed to suppress it? Until everything exploded and she fled impulsively into the unknown?

How had it happened? How had she remained married to a man she was no longer even friends with, woken up each morning next to another sleeping human being and not understood how lonely she was? He lay there like a big whale or bear, nothing more than a symbol that she wasn't alone. The unabashed bodily noises and the acts of sex four times a month were only a sort of testimony to having been together for a long time. So why did she even care that she found out yesterday that he'd been leading a parallel life? That her own life with him was not even real, despite unabashed habits and their family life?

Her life had not been for real!

She drove her car to the university, worked late, went to lectures, wrote and researched, and somewhere in all this he'd disappeared. And somewhere she stopped being that talented young woman who wrote papers and textbooks. Instead, she was now a slightly drunk forty-eight year old lady, sitting in economy class on a flight across the Atlantic.

She ordered more wine.

Noted objectively that the flight attendant didn't even lift an eyebrow over the fact that the well-dressed lady in a beige suit, sitting in 16A was now on her third little bottle of Merlot. *After* a Bloody Mary.

Was this what being middle-aged was like? Getting drunk on airplanes?

There had once been another Alice, she thought as she balanced the small wine glass in her palm. Indeed! A bubbly, curious Alice; a child who crawled around in flower beds and took apart leaves and flowers to see how ingeniously they were constructed. A child who lay on the rug in her parents' living room and studied city maps for hours; who marveled at the lack of system, that no one had thought out and planned any overall scheme before the city had been built. She, Alice the child, had cut off Tantolunden, replaced it with parts of Hjorthagen. Organized the buildings. And really enjoyed the improvements after *she* rebuilt the map.

And now that she was middle-aged, she was an authority in her field, a person who wrote books. Someone who mattered.

But her life was not for real!

She downed her drink. Ignored the stares from the lady across the aisle.

Laughed suddenly.

Loudly.

To just leave—like this. She always planned everything in detail. Always. Always. She looked around quickly but the lady across the aisle was buried in her book and no one else seemed to notice that she was sitting there laughing out loud to herself.

Tipsy.

She reached down for her purse on the floor. Opened her wallet, took out a photograph. Looked at it for a long time, as if she'd never seen the picture properly before. They had similar skin tone and hair color. But her daughter's eyes were different, introverted and dreamlike. Babylonia had always been softer, was different inside. As a child, she'd claimed that she heard choirs singing in the dark. Chanting voices inside her head. Alice had wanted to reassure her, and resolutely cut up a cod's head to show her what was there behind the forehead, under the scales and slime. The child's eyes had widened in wonder over the scientific discovery. That the cod head did not, as she'd imagined, contain any tangible thoughts. And she'd thrown the fish against the wall.

Funny!

She put the photo away and looked out at the gray mass of clouds, felt the chilly windowpane against her forehead. She would just have to try and enjoy floating around way up here, in the world that you're in when you fly. Where everything stands still and the only thing you can do is to be. It was what it was.

And she thought she sensed something moving among the clouds, wished it would prove to be an angel.

And it was a new and inexplicably pleasant idea, to sit on the inside of a small window and look out at a thick mass of water—a cloud—and wish it were possible that there really was an angel out there.

* * *

Meanwhile, the city she was on her way to had come to life and spit its residents out of their cramped apartments, down into the subway and onto the streets where they poured into office buildings. Thousands of chrome colored elevators transported passengers up and down, workers rushing between cubicles through office landscapes, folders in hand and calendars filled with appointments and meetings.

And on Mulberry Street in Little Italy, a man stepped out of a building. He was dressed in a gray old-style European suit, complete with vest and tie. Long sideburns framed his oblong Flemish face. In his left hand, he held the tail end of a cigarette, and before he began to walk toward Spring Street, he lit a new one from the butt. His name is Charles, and he's around forty-five years old. More about him in a moment.

2

Without waking Gabor, Babylonia put on a simple black cotton dress. She slipped quietly out of the apartment, hurried across the Bowery and walked, bag swinging, through Chinatown up to Little Italy to have breakfast by herself, her step so much lighter than it was with him at her side. Both of them had a show tonight. He worked the lights, she the box office. As volunteers, of course, but it was a way of gaining experience. And experience was hard currency in life.

The sweltering August heat had lain like a damp cloth over the city. Now, the heat has finally broken. She took a deep breath and enjoyed the hint of freshness in the air.

A little ways up Mulberry Street, she sat down at a small rickety table in an outdoor cafe and ordered cappuccino and a sandwich. She knew that they sliced the cheese thinly at this place. And that you could get whole grain bread. If you asked for it.

While she waited for her coffee, she studied a girl who sat reading at the next table. Dark, with thick, well-shaped eyebrows. Her long slender legs were stretched in front of her, wound around a soft suede bag in nut brown. How would it feel to lie naked under a blanket next to her? Feel her soft body instead of Gabor's hard one?

Hands touching breasts, hips, the taste of the same sex? She felt strangely aroused, and embarrassed. Turned her gaze toward a middle-aged man, face framed in huge sideburns, who was reading at another table. She studied his mature hands rolling a cigarette, expertly and a bit absentmindedly. Felt an urge to touch him. To stroke his veined hand with her finger. But what kind of person was she who could be honest neither with herself nor with the man she loved? Because she did love Gabor—she just didn't want to live with him anymore, she wanted to see what else life had to offer. And she believed it was her right, even though she was ashamed of the thought as she bit into her sandwich. But she would never dare to sleep with the girl with the beautiful eyebrows or the man with the cigarette and the long sideburns.

Lately, she'd become more and more obsessed with the idea that she was simply so tediously ordinary. Had relocated to the other side of the globe and then just chosen what felt safe: part-time work at a Swedish export company, volunteer job in the evenings at a third-class off-off-Broadway theater. Now she was sitting here watching a man's veined hands, following the contours of a beautiful girl's legs—realizing that the adventure she was looking for might well be sitting there right in front of her. But her ordinariness was becoming a prison. Her timidity a locked door. She didn't even have the courage to go into a bar by herself.

God, she was so tired of herself.

We glide through the exhaust-filled, humid summer air, across the street, up the facade of a narrow brick building, to an open window on the fifth floor, where a sixty-three-year-old opera singer in cobalt blue silk pajamas is watching the guests at the outdoor cafe.

He feels slightly aroused but also a bit envious as he watches the girl down there voraciously wolfing down her sandwich. She's got some appetite. An appetite for food, an appetite for life, he thinks. She undoubtedly sees clear possibilities when she meets her own reflection. Not like himself: uglier by the day; more loathsome. He never imagined that aging could be this horrible when he was the girl's age. And he *very* sincerely, *fervently*, would like to wish that she'll be spared. That she'll simply be blessed with continuing to be young and hungry, filled with desire. But jealousy gets the upper hand and he can't help thinking, "Just wait... soon you'll be like me. It happens so quickly, you see. Faster than you think." Leisurely, but very deliberately, he reaches out the window, wants her to know that he exists. He looks up at the clear, blue sky, opens his mouth and starts practicing the first scales of the day. He doesn't dare look down to see if she appears to hear him.

We leave him, for the moment—up there in his cobalt blue pajamas on the fifth floor of the brick building on the Italian street—to continue our story.

3

Gabor had slept most of the day. Called Babylonia at work when he woke up but she had just left.

He stepped clumsily out of the tub and wrapped a frayed, tattered towel around his waist. Sighed in disappointment as he looked down at the empty coffee can. Opened the fridge, stared at the desolation in there, took out a bruised banana. Sat down on a wooden chair at the kitchen window, bit into the disgusting gooey banana, and stared pensively out the window at the gray wall of the building across the way.

Meanwhile, a bus pulled out from Newark Airport. It made its way slowly toward the highway and continued through a landscape of marshes filled with wrecked cars and train remnants. Alice sat on the hard seat and watched an incomprehensible world; so ugly and full of apocalyptic desolation, despite the heavy traffic. Was this the right direction?

But on the horizon, the city's contours began to emerge through the yellow haze. Passengers pressed their noses against the bus windows and saw how these contours surrealistically resembled all the pictures and paintings. They leaned back in their seats and watched the city. While Alice closed her eyes and fell asleep—finally.

A small, overweight man dressed in a tight, plaid shirt sat next to Alice. He watched the classy Scandinavian lady who was sleeping so peacefully, her lips slightly parted. Her purse lay open on her lap. Through the opening, he saw a thick wallet in dark brown leather. Feeling protective of the foreign lady, he gently leaned over and closed her bag. His eye met those of an elderly woman across the aisle who had seen what he'd done.

She nodded encouragingly.

He winked back.

And they smiled at one another. Silently.

* * *

Babylonia pushed the door open. Stepped into the darkness and opened the small mailbox. It was empty except for a few flyers which she left there. Carrying a heavy grocery bag in each hand, she opened the inner door and cursed the many stairs that she had to climb. Thought decisively that *NOW* she would talk to him. She had to. But as she climbed the stairs, the steps felt twice as steep as usual, as if they were growing as she climbed.

The stink of cat pee permeated the stairwell. On one floor, she heard a rooster crow. Despite the fact that it sometimes woke her at the crack of dawn, Babylonia found the crowing kind of homey. There must be a dozen people living in the apartment with the rooster. She didn't understand how they all fit. She had the feeling that they worked and slept in shifts. At any time of day, someone was coming out of the apartment down the stairs or someone was on their way up the stairs toward home. It always smelled of cooking. The day never ended. Someone was sleeping, someone was starting his day, someone else's day was just ending. But the rooster followed the natural rhythm of the day. He slept when it was dark and crowed at dawn.

* * *

When Gabor heard footsteps on the stairs he stood up. Had to get dressed. Knew she'd want him to have gotten up, grabbed hold of the day. Not slept in. But he had failed—again.

He hurried out of the room, looking for his cigarettes. Smoothed the sheets on the bed so that it looked made and opened the tiny bedroom window that looked out on the shaft of the building next door. Pigeons cooed out there. He turned toward his underwear drawer while he listened to the sound of the approaching footsteps on the stairs.

* * *

Babylonia stopped outside the door. Listened, but it was quiet in there. She tried her key in the rickety police lock … not locked.

Inside the apartment, both cats greeted her at the door. She put down her bags, picked up the cat food and poured some into two bowls. The cats hissed at each other. She left her grocery bags on the bench, took off her shoes and placed them prudently near the door, peeked into the next room. Gabor was standing there, naked, rooting around his underwear drawer. All his underpants were falling apart. He said a gloomy hello as he continued to inspect a crotch seam that was beyond repair.

She stopped at the door, feeling increasingly annoyed. He still wasn't dressed even though the day was almost over.

Why don't you buy a new pair," she snapped, leaning forward and peering down into his drawer. The small collection of dingy underwear depressed her.

Gabor said nothing. Just stood there, hairy and naked, with an unlit cigarette in his mouth.

"Do me a favor and light that cigarette. It looks so pretentious just hanging unlit like that."

Gabor turned slowly towards her, took the cigarette out of his mouth and put it behind his ear. It instantly fell off and rolled away towards the cats. Without looking at her he murmured quietly, "Where have you been? I tried you at work."

"Food shopping."

"What took so long? You left work at three-thirty."

"I took the subway, I bought food, I carried the bags home. What the hell do you think I did?"

"I don't know. How should I know what you do when you're not at work?" He took a new cigarette out of the pack. Lit it. Left the other on the floor.

She picked up the cigarette from the floor. Gathered her courage.

"I'm going to look at an apartment in Queens tomorrow."

Now it was said. She felt relieved and sat down on the bed. Gabor bit the new cigarette so hard it broke.

"Queens? What's wrong with living here? Who wants to live in Queens?"

To avoid looking at him, she bent down and picked up the worn towel he had thrown on the floor and hung it on a chair. The towel smelled sour. He, however, smelled pleasantly of soap mixed with that special scent that was just his. The scent that used to make her completely languid.

She replied shortly, "I want to try living on my own."

He turned away. "Oh! Just like that?"

His neck and wide shoulders slumped and she almost changed her mind. Reluctantly felt tenderness poison her determination. Wanted to go over and touch him.

Wished she wanted to.

How had it come to be this tedious?

Not just like that!" His scent filled the room insistently making her weak at the knees. She snorted hard to avoid breathing it in.

"Sounds that way..."

She tried to change the tone. "Please, babe, I can't hear you with that cigarette in your mouth. Take it out."

Gabor spat out the last bit of cigarette. "You don't understand anything. You come home and set bombs off all around you. Queens!" Amazingly, he already had a new unlit cigarette in his hand. "I might have stomach ulcers. Don't you get it? I've been in bed all day."

She should go over and hug him. Shouldn't be so angry all the time. But how could you live with someone who makes your skin crawl? Not only that, he should understand how courageous it was of her to consider living on her own, in a part of the city where no one else really lives. No one they knew.

She sat on the bed and tried to figure out how to explain this to him. He had come here as a refugee in 1982. Sure, that was sad—and true. A reality she couldn't grasp or understand. He simply had no homeland to return to. While she had just come here out of curiosity from a Sweden she could move back to anytime she wanted. So his gloominess was definitely justified. Absolutely. But still...

She sighed and was about to try again, but he beat her to it, nodded toward the black answering machine on the floor.

"Someone left a message on the machine."

She stood up, walked over to the machine and bent down. "Well, who was it?"

"A woman. It's no longer there."

She pressed the buttons. Nothing.

"Wait... you erased it?"

"No, *I* didn't erase it. *Your* cat did."

Elvis was lying on the couch next to her, calmly licking his paws.

She suppressed her anger and concentrated on the dead answering machine even though she knew it was hopeless.

Why was everything so difficult? Would love ever get easier?

Gabor continued accusingly, mumbling, as he lit the cigarette. "Your cat is so hyper. Really crazy. He pulled out the cord while he was chasing, like... nothing."

"But who was it?"

"I don't know," he said and walked naked toward the window. His penis was hanging morosely between his powerful thighs.

"Sounded like Swedish. But I didn't recognize the voice."

Babylonia pressed the buttons again—but there was still nothing there. Gabor put his hand on his stomach and sighed deeply as he blew smoke through the open window.

"Well, please, get dressed," she hissed.

He remained at the window.

I'm changing, she thought, becoming someone I don't like. Her parents never quarreled; they've been living together for twenty years. How did they do it?

* * *

A little later, when the light began to disappear behind the roofs, when the sun's rays no longer lit up the corners of the small apartment and all the shabbiness became softer and easier to ignore, Gabor lay on the couch, his stomach still aching. So fragile, despite his big body. He had twisted his already curly hair around his finger so that it resembled sprawling dreads, or as if someone had plugged him into an electrical outlet that caused his hair to stick out like steel spirals.

Babylonia was standing in the doorway with a bottle of Pepto-Bismol in her hand, looking at him. What would it be like to bring him to Äppelviken? A Tolkien giant home to the Shire. Get off the metro at Alvik, stop at the supermarket. He would stand there—the giant—and gloomily scrutinize the buttermilk, crispbread, the local headlines with advice from the government about six slices of bread a day. He would comment on everything with that melancholy Hungarian sense of humor she first fell in love with. She smiled at the thought, and he saw the smile and gave her a hurt look.

"It wasn't about you," she whispered, and poured the thick, neon pink liquid from the Pepto-Bismol bottle into a spoon.

"Here. Drink up. You have to start getting dressed."

She was too young for this.

4

The diesel-fogged airport bus reached its final destination, the top level of the gigantic bus terminal in mid-Manhattan. The passengers got off, picked up their luggage, and proceeded to the labyrinth of elevators and escalators that would take them down to the street and waiting taxis.

Alice was one of the last people to get off the bus. She had been awakened by an overweight man wearing a tight plaid shirt. She turned away quickly, embarrassed by the stale taste of sleep and alcohol in her mouth. Now she stood alone outside the bus and looked around. Wanted to get out of there. Ideally, to go back home, but that was impossible. She was on this side of the Atlantic. Stranded, lost—on the top floor of a gray bus terminal filled with desolate noises and gasoline fumes.

That was the simple reality.

She turned to the bus driver who was still sitting behind the wheel engrossed in the baseball scores in his newspaper.

"Excuse me," she said quietly. The small words, uttered faintly in proper Oxford English, had no effect whatsoever.

"Excuse me," she tried again a little louder. "Where are all the porers?"

"Porters?" Now he looked up, smiled politely and shook his head. "Sorry, little lady, as you can see there are no porters here. Not right now, anyway."

He glanced at her bag. A nice leather suitcase from Palmgren's. It was a present for her fortieth birthday. It was quite impractical, had no wheels and was very heavy, but she thought it was infinitely beautiful. She loved it, but it required assistance, a porter, a luggage cart. And here, high up in the gigantic bus terminal, there wasn't a porter or luggage cart in sight.

"I'd be careful if I were you," the driver continued amicably. "Don't let anyone help you with the bag if they're not wearing a uniform."

He yawned and went back to his baseball scores.

Alice looked around. The exit was a good ways off. Nevertheless, she declined help from a young black teenager who had suddenly appeared beside her and taken hold of her bag. She snatched the bag and dragged it towards the exit. The guy chased after her.

"Wait, lady, my name is Mister Man. Do you need some help? Lady..."

He did not give up. She quickened her step. He looked no older than fourteen or fifteen.

"I'm Mister Man. Lady, I AM Mister Man. At your service."

He had on baggy jeans that looked like they were about to fall off; she noticed that he kept stepping on the hems. She stopped and looked him straight in the eye.

"You should pull up your pants. Look... you're ruining them."

He stared at her in surprise.

"Uh, what?"

"Your pants, can't you see that they're falling apart. At the bottom."

He looked down at his chalk-white sneakers that were sticking out from under the wide pant legs. But when he saw that the lady had begun moving toward the escalator, he ran after her again.

"Mister Man wants to help. Come on, let me have the bag."

Alice had never been to New York. Had not traveled much at all really—only a bit for work. Her one exotic destination had been Bombay for a five-day academic conference. The dirt and chaos here at the bus station in Manhattan reminded her of that trip. Or was it the smell combined with the heat, exhaust fumes, unwashed bodies? There was definitely something here that reminded her of those five days in Bombay.

She turned to Mister Man who was hanging about her on the escalator and going on about how she should let him carry her bag and get her a taxi. She interrupted him in the middle of his chatter.

"Just like Bombay."

He picked up on that immediately. "Bombay? Sixth Street? I can help you get a cab. Mister Man is always ready to help."

He continued following her as she went down escalator after escalator—further and further down—until she was outside the terminal in a taxi line on Eighth Avenue and Forty-first Street.

Mister Man pulled open a taxi door with a big smile and made sure her bag ended up in the trunk. She looked at his outstretched hand, bewildered. The cab driver muttered something under his breathed, pushed the boy away and closed the cab door. But Mister Man did not give up. He knocked on the window.

"Hey. Mister Man can go with you lady. Show you where Bombay is. I want to help."

She rummaged in her purse and found the smallest bill she had in her stack of new US dollars, a crisp five-dollar-bill. She rolled down the window and handed it to him. He looked down at the money, shrugged and looked around for the next potential customer.

Through the taxi's dusty window, Alice looked at the broad avenue. If you counted the cars parked on either side, the street was six lanes wide. And everywhere there were people, cars, bumps and potholes.

She slipped around on the slick vinyl seat, felt both nervous and... a little happy. Happy? Was that something she could still feel? Or was it simply that this city seemed so unreal that the pain she felt yesterday hadn't yet caught up with her? Maybe it was somewhere over the Atlantic like a seedy cloud, chasing her? But it wasn't here at the moment. Not yet.

The taxi turned onto 6th Street, stopped outside a place where pink neon lights flashed B-o-m-b-a-y. She looked out at the row of Indian restaurants that lined the street. The smells of curry, cloves, coriander, roast lamb and garlic filled the cab. She realized what had happened and knocked on the divider between herself and the driver.

"But this is wrong. I'm going to Chinatown."

The cab driver turned around and gave her a long, annoyed look.

"Chinatown," she repeated. "Catherine Street."

He turned away and started the car again.

"Fucking foreigners," she heard him mutter in a thick Russian accent.

She leaned back and looked out at the street that contained so much of India. Shimmering lights in the windows, the smell of cardamom and garam masala, colorful posters of gods and artists, squiggly symbols she didn't understand. And other, ordinary letters, which formed exotic names like Madras, Punjab and Bombay.

When the taxi turned the corner she was back in America again. Now slummier, more worn out. They drove down another broad avenue, passing cars with lots of scratches and dents; the law of the jungle apparently applied to parking here. Dogs were poking about in the garbage outside a food stall. A heavy bass rhythm boomed from a huge radio that stood on the roof of a parked car. On a side street, she caught a glimpse of kids running through the water spurting from a fire hydrant, chased by a half-naked shaggy man. A bicycle messenger in tight red shorts whizzed past her taxi and kept switching lanes in the heavy traffic like a kamikaze pilot.

"Fucking foreigners," muttered the driver again in his Russian accent, and she realized that for the first time in the past twenty-four hours, she was actually smiling.

* * *

The shrill, hard sound of the intercom reverberated through the small apartment making Babylonia flinch and drop her contact lens.

"Who is it? No! Are you expecting someone?" Gabor stuck his head into the bathroom. As always, he was reluctant to let anyone in, just as unwilling as he was to answer the phone if he wasn't prepared. He first wanted to know who and why...

He bent over her, happy to ignore the intercom.

"Need help?"

"I dropped my contact lens into the toilet. Dammit." She was bent over the toilet seat, glasses perched on her nose again, trying to find the little transparent plastic disc down there in the water. How could something so small be so important?

He sat down next to her.

"In the toilet? Huh?"

She started to giggle. "What do I do now?"

He leaned forward. Brushed away a lock of hair from her eye. Tenderly. Wanted to be close to her. For everything to return to normal. As if no one had mentioned an apartment in Queens. Or moving there.

But the shrill sound of the intercom cut through the apartment again—three urgent rings.

"Do me a favor and open the door," she snapped.

"Hello, who's there?" she heard him say sullenly from the kitchen, mumbling, with as dismissive a voice as he could muster.

There was no answer.

"Hello, is anyone there?"

She was about to get up and answer it herself when the intercom crackled, sounds from the street mixed with a woman's voice, loud and shrill in the finest Oxford English.

"Is this the right place?"

Gabor sighed.

"The right place? For what?"

Silence. You could hear a car passing below. And then—the woman's voice again. This time slowly and deliberately.

"Does Babylonia live here?"

Alice hadn't dared put down her suitcase. The dirty pavement stank of garbage and disgusting, exotic spices. Whole birds hung upside down in the shop window next to Babylonia's building. Strange looking vegetables were displayed on a brown bench outside the shop. The shop owner was closing up for the day. A boy came out to bring in the vegetables and a short skinny Asian woman just missed Alice's feet when she poured out a bucket of smelly water on the pavement directly outside the shop.

Babylonia finally found the lens, flushed it in saline solution and popped it into her eye, praying to God that the eye wouldn't become infected.

Gabor appeared again at the bathroom door.

"Do you know anyone named Alice?"

She blinked so that the lens would lodge properly.

"No, I don't know any Alice. You know that. You know everyone I..."

She stopped mid-sentence. But it couldn't be. Could it? She rushed out to the intercom.

* * *

After the first hug, they were both completely silent as they climbed up the five flights of stairs. It stank of cat pee.

At first, Alice hadn't recognized her daughter in this unfamiliar context. Was startled when she saw her pale face through the door pane. As they passed the third floor, she heard something that sounded like a rooster crowing.

"A rooster?" she asked, mostly as a joke. After all, people don't keep roosters *inside* their apartments. But Babylonia didn't answer. She struggled, carrying the heavy Palmgren suitcase in both hands, a deep crease between her eyebrows.

Once they were in the apartment, they hugged awkwardly again. Alice looked around over her daughter's soft hair. There was no hallway, you just stepped straight into the kitchen where an ugly old porcelain bathtub stood in plain sight. Through the kitchen window, she saw the gray wall of the building next door. A narrow shaft between the buildings was all there was.

She released her daughter and greeted a tall young man who had emerged from another room. His hair was in ringlets that stuck out in all directions like electric coils. He hadn't shaved and was wearing a pair of shorts although it was autumn. His muscular chest was covered by a faded T-shirt with just the word "NO" in green lettering. He greeted her gloomily with a kiss on the cheek, catching her by surprise as she offered her hand. The kiss landed somewhat off target, too close to her mouth. They stepped apart, feeling immediately uncomfortable with one another.

Babylonia hadn't gathered her thoughts yet. Why had her mother just turned up? Without calling first. What would they do now? She couldn't formulate the questions she wanted to ask. Too shaken. Didn't want Sweden and her mother to step into her life without giving her time to prepare.

She saw her mother look critically about. And for the first time, through her mother's eyes, she saw how shabby the place must look. The dirt in the corners that couldn't be cleaned. Kitchen chairs that Gabor had found in the trash on the street. The paint-flaked walls. She took the roach trap that stood by the sink and discreetly moved it behind the dishwashing liquid. Peered over to see if her mother noticed, but her mother was busy petting Elvis who'd come in from the other room with an angry meow.

"It must be nice to be a cat here," Alice said to Gabor with a smile. "A lot of mice, right?"

Gabor turned away, offended. "We don't have any mice."

Alice seemed not to hear. She pointed at Loser who was hiding under the kitchen table.

"Another one. Good lord, what a fat cat. Are these your cats, honey?"

She turned to Babylonia who, though not wanting to sound annoyed, heard herself answer more sharply than she meant to, "No, Mom. That's Gabor's cat. Only the black one is mine. Elvis. As you well know. I've sent pictures."

Alice couldn't remember receiving a picture of a black cat, but felt it wasn't appropriate to say that right then. Instead, she turned to Gabor and said loudly, slowly and as clearly as she could in her proper university English. "What an enormous cat. That is probably why you have no mice, right?"

"Mom," said Babylonia quickly in Swedish. "He's not an imbecile."

Gabor stared at the cats. Looked like he was searching for words, as if the cats would come up with something he could say.

"Would you like something to drink," he finally asked, and without waiting for an answer, he took some glasses out of the cupboard and ice from the freezer. He grabbed the ice with his hand and put it in the glasses, without using a spoon, ice tongs or any other implement. Poured in the remains of an opened bottle of Sauvignon Blanc.

Alice brushed her finger discreetly over the rim of her glass; she could see it was cracked. Noticed that her daughter was irritated, that Babylonia snatched back the glass and handed over her own instead.

"Mom, you can't just show up like this. What are we going to do now?"

Alice felt the joy of arrival begin to turn into panic. Began sweating profusely, wiped her forehead nervously. Suddenly, she wanted to turn around and step back over the threshold into the house in Äppelviken, travel back in time and undo finding the slip of paper in Göran's pocket. The one that had kicked off this entire trip.

"Aren't you at all pleased to see me?" was all she could manage to say.

Babylonia flipped back her hair in an annoyed gesture. The long strawberry blond hair that Alice had braided so neatly when Babylonia was a child. She wanted to caress it now but felt embarrassed that she'd just shown up like this. What had she been thinking?

Babylonia came a little closer.

"Mom, of course I'm glad you're here. Very glad. It's just very strange. How could you just hop a plane over the Atlantic without letting me know?"

"I... wanted to surprise you. It was all quite last minute. I'll explain later."

She glanced at Gabor. "I'm going to look for a hotel nearby. I just wanted to stop by and say hello first. Don't want to be a bother."

She put her hand on her daughter's shoulder. "Has your father called?" Felt her daughter tense up.

"Why would he have called?"

"I thought maybe..."

She took a sip of wine from the glass with the unsanitary ice.

"I called you from the airport."

Babylonia glanced at the answering machine that still lay on the floor unplugged.

"Something doesn't add up, Mom. What's happened?"

Alice was unable to explain. Was unable to do anything. As if a hundred pound rucksack suddenly hung on her shoulders. Just wanted to sit down. But the wooden chairs looked hard and uncomfortable. She hadn't imagined that her daughter would be living with someone. Hadn't thought at all—just hopped on a plane. How foolish!

She turned to Gabor.

"I'll merely be visiting for a few days. I can stay at a hotel."

"Lovely to have you here. You're welcome to stay with us. Stay as long as you'd like."

Alice missed the irony in his voice. Turned to her daughter again and said, almost pleading, "See that. He thinks it's lovely... That's nice of him."

She lowered her voice and continued in Swedish.

"I didn't know you had a roommate. Is he your boyfriend? Why haven't you said anything?"

Babylonia was painfully aware that she should have patience with a mother who showed up completely unexpected. But she felt she just couldn't cope with the mother who was standing here now. In her kitchen. Without warning. Who didn't remember that her own daughter had told her that she lived with a boyfriend. Didn't even remember that she had a black cat.

And yet, just showing up like this was so unlike her mother. She planned their vacations a year in advance and had them celebrate Christmas and Easter in exactly the same way, year after year. In Babylonia's experience, there was never any room for improvisation in her mother's life. Something big, something disruptive and difficult must be behind this unannounced voyage across the Atlantic.

She approached her mother, wanted to touch her, but simply said, "You're welcome to stay here, Mom. Gabor's mother will be visiting from Budapest in about a month, so it's sort of fair. It's Gabor's apartment, actually."

And that wasn't at all what she'd wanted to say.

She was afraid to find out what it was that had made her mother just get on a plane. She wanted to ask—but not now. They had to get going.

Could she get someone to fill in for her? Send Gabor by himself? But he couldn't manage both the box office and the lights. She had to go; she wasn't irresponsible, like some people.

Alice looked towards Gabor and said quietly in Swedish, "He's very big for a Hungarian. I thought they were small and dark. If his mother's the same size, you'll barely all fit in here."

Babylonia sighed and took Alice's hand.

"Mom, really..."

No one said anything for several interminable seconds. Gabor stood with an unlit cigarette in one hand, his other hand over his stomach. Rigid. He held out his pack of cigarettes to Alice, who flinched and pointed to the bathtub next to the stove and addressed Babylonia in Swedish, whispering as if Gabor could understand.

"Why do you have a bathtub in the kitchen? Is that really sanitary?"

Babylonia didn't respond.

Just took a couple of deep breaths.

The silence spread across the kitchen like leaking gas, paralyzing them all. They stood isolated within themselves but sharing the same uneasiness, thick and heavy. Gabor, who didn't understand what either woman had said, smiled. Wanted to do the right thing. Drew a deep drag on his cigarette with his hand pointed on his stomach.

"Do you like jazz?" he asked, suddenly perking up. He went into the bedroom and the sound of a desolate but energetic saxophone solo soon filled the apartment.

Alice peered into the room. It was a small windowless walk-through room that they used as a bedroom. The big hairy guy sat on the bed rocking back and forth to the music.

Babylonia followed Alice into the room, walked over to the stereo and lowered the volume. Led her mother into the apartment's other room, which was a bit larger and with windows that faced the street.

"We have to work tonight. Both of us. Will you be OK on your own for a few hours? We work at a small theater on 13th Street—just a few hours—we'll come right home afterwards—do you think you can manage to sleep on the couch tonight?"

Alice touched her daughter's arm.

"It's fine. Of course I'll manage!" She looked at the black vinyl couch that dominated the narrow room. "That's a really a big sofa.

How did you get it up here?"

"Will you be okay on your own here a few hours?" Babylonia repeated without commenting on her mother's question. Because she couldn't tell her the story of the couch. That it had been in the apartment when Gabor moved in. If Alice found out that it wasn't new, that there might have been a brothel here before Gabor moved in, or a home for illegal Asian immigrants who toiled in secret garment factories, that anything could have taken place on that smooth vinyl couch, that it could be housing cockroaches or a family of mice, that someone could have been killed or conceived on it—that you simply had to put up with the egregious fact of having a questionable vinyl couch imposed on you if you wanted to live in this city; if Alice had divined all that, would she have agreed to sleep on this couch of vinyl?

Never.

Not her mother.

Alice wanted to leave, look for a hotel. A comfortable bed. She felt paralyzed by fatigue; it must be way past midnight back home in Sweden.

A tornado had blown into her life, blown her halfway around the earth, and she had not rested. Now everything stopped. And it had all turned out so wrong.

"Don't worry about me," she said. "All I want to do right now is sleep. Tomorrow I can find a nice hotel."

She looked around.

"I can make up the couch and go to sleep. I'll see you tomorrow. We can talk some more then."

Babylonia turned around—went back to her mother and took her hand gently in her own. "It's great having you here. I'll get some sheets."

Alice hugged her.

"We'll have a proper talk tomorrow... I'm exhausted... you know what I mean."

Babylonia went to the bathroom to get ready. Gabor followed.

"Why is she staying here?" he whispered and squeezed in beside her.

"Please. I don't know what she's doing here. My mother never shows up unannounced like this. Ever."

"She doesn't feel like a mother. More like a British museum curator."

"She's a professor."

"A professor of what?" he asked and stood to pee. She quickly pulled the door shut.

"Something to do with human behavior, structures, systemic knowledge."

Gabor shuddered and shook his penis dry.

"Creepy."

* * *

A moment later they hurried up the deserted street. Storefronts were dark and fitted with gray metal gates blocking the view both in and out. Gabor took Babylonia's hand as usual. She glanced up at the window where she sensed Alice looking down at them.

She pulled her hand out of his tight grip and pretended to look for something in her pocket to hide the fact that she didn't want him to hold her hand. He gave her a hurt look. She felt guilty and snuck her hand under his arm so that they walked arm-in-arm, like two friends.

* * *

Alice saw them hurrying down the street. She felt a combination of tenderness and perhaps a bit of envy that her daughter was still young, light on her feet and seemed to be enjoying her life.

She leaned her forehead against the windowpane and just stood there for a moment, didn't want the feeling from earlier this morning in Sweden to catch up with her quite yet. How long had her husband been a stranger to her?

She had a vague memory of intimacy, warmth—but it was as if it were about other people. Not him and her.

For years they had lived together in intimacy based on family ties, on owning a house. On the bed where they had sex once a week or so, year after year. Even though it had mostly become a routine fuck by now. But is it really possible that he had come home and slept with her after he had been with another woman—or women? There must have been more than one.

In Berlin, of all places.

How could she have been so fooled?

She caressed her stomach, cupped a breast in her hand. She might be a little too skinny, but that meant that her skin and breasts were still firm. Still, how could she compete with the child he was having a relationship with? Why should he want her?

She sat down and looked around the small oblong room.

The apartment was like a small train, she thought; it began in the kitchen, followed by the tiny bedroom, where there was only room for the unmade bed, and ended in the room with the couch where she was sitting now.

She stood up and peered into the bedroom again. A pack of cigarettes and an empty beer bottle stood on an inverted beer crate that served as the bedside table. Could they not afford to buy furniture?

Or is this what happens when two people have their families in another continent? It suddenly struck her that her daughter was an immigrant in this country. Someone who couldn't inherit furniture from her relatives.

The stereo was high up on a shelf. There was hardly any space left around the bed apart from the passage that led to the kitchen. A black and white poster from a movie called *The Attack of the 50-Foot Woman* was the only decoration. A giant woman wearing a bikini holding a small man in her fist. It was neither funny nor beautiful. And not political either. Just completely incomprehensible. Whose poster was it? Why?

She turned again toward the room facing the street. It, too, was narrow and messy. The worn vinyl couch she was supposed to sleep on was held together with duct tape on one side. Several volumes of Hesse and Boris Vian were on the bookshelf. She smiled in recognition. Remembered her own youthful desire years ago to manifest being well-read with those very same books. She went over and stroked the spines. Saw a Russian translation of *Alice in Wonderland*. Nabokov's translation. Picked up the book, looked at the familiar illustrations, here in beautiful Russian lettering.

In the middle of the bookshelf stood a five-liter wine bottle with a screw cap. She had never before seen such a large one, examined it closely. Yes, it definitely was wine, from New York State.

She went into the kitchen and fetched a glass and with great difficulty carefully poured a glass of wine from the unwieldy bottle. It tasted sweet and cheap, not pleasant and crisp like the good wines she was accustomed to, but she sipped at it anyway.

Somewhere in the building, the rooster crowed again. It didn't sound like a TV rooster but rather a real one. And it sounded nearby.

She returned to the window that faced the street. The rooster had stopped crowing. She leaned her forehead against the cool windowpane again and looked out at the factory across the street. Where people sat and sewed. It looked nice. They worked, had somewhere they belonged.

How long had she focused solely on her career? Deep, deep inside was a little hungry, lustful, erotic girl—another Alice, like an echo from a previous life. She had assumed that this part of her didn't exist at all anymore. That she was content. But Göran—he had not been content. Was it human? She closed her eyes. Yes, she thought it was human. But not necessarily fair. And she saw no solution. There was no solution. Just a bleak sadness that life had simply whizzed past and here she stood, middle-aged without really understanding how it had happened. Without having lived. She had just existed. Without the joy of living others seemed to have: the neighbors on the other side of the fence in Äppelviken with their loud music, their children running around unsupervised in the garden playing noisily at the most peculiar times of day. All the drunken dinners that she had studied from her side of the fence, from under her sunhat, behind her sunglasses.

The thought struck her that those other people—her neighbors, her husband, the idiots on TV soaps—those people might have realized something about life that she had missed, that her choices in life had stood in the way of something as basic as a primitive lust for life.

But no, she most certainly had once felt a lust for life. She had loved. She had enjoyed sex, good food, a beautifully worded sentence. But she had also grown complacent. Or just kept going. And now here she was, and the train that was her life had gotten stuck, or had taken a wrong turn, or maybe it simply had switched to another track—a track that led nowhere.

She took another sip of wine, looked down on the window lock—an old-style design that resembled nothing she had seen in Sweden. You push up the lower pane so that it lay in front of the top one. Outside, there was a large fire escape with landings at each story. She pushed open the window. It was easy. Tested the fire escape gently. It felt less rickety than she had imagined.

Basil and parsley were growing in pots on the fire escape. There was also a cushion to sit on. How healthy could it be to grow herbs here with all the exhaust fumes? At home, she grew basil, thyme, sage—the scent of rosemary rose from the flowerbed outside the kitchen door. The air in the garden in Äppelviken was clean and fresh; the Nordic sun provided just the right amount of sunlight and the spices were given ample time to mature slowly and tasted heavenly, harvested directly from the garden. But here? In the dirt? With all the fumes? She and Babylonia must make the time to have a proper talk tomorrow.

Wine glass in hand, she stepped cautiously onto the fire escape, sat down on the cushion and looked down at the street. Felt a bit better. It was certainly dirty, but so different from anything she had ever experienced that she didn't really care about the dirt.

Sitting on a fire escape in Chinatown and looking down at the street and the buildings and the smell of the big city that really wasn't scary at all, but rather warmly welcoming—it was... she couldn't find the right expression though the simple little word exciting almost fit the bill.

But it was more than just exciting. It was like an erotic feeling that began to spread through her body. She almost shuddered to think that she actually dared to sit in her well-ironed suit on a dirty cushion on a fire escape that was black from soot and fumes.

Maybe—if only no one bothered her. If she didn't have to explain what happened. Didn't have to think about it, explain, analyze—then she'd be able to survive this.

Down on the street, a life was unfolding that was completely unlike anything she had seen before. A young Asian couple was having trouble starting their car. They quarreled in a rattling fast Chinese dialect.

Further up the desolate street, came a tall, lanky man—from her vantage point, he looked like he could be close to two meters tall. He walked with long strides toward the bar at the corner. His pants were too short and his entire body was oversized, like a giant's. The bar's windows were dirty and dark but he waved anyway to someone inside, opened the door and disappeared into obscurity after being forced to bow his head to get through the door—or did he? Maybe he didn't bend at all. Maybe he wasn't a giant. She wasn't sure. Right now, everything looked a little stranger than usual through her new eyes.

The rickety black iron fire escape went all the way up to the roof. She stood up and, a bit wobbly, started climbing the steep stairs. She looked down between steps for a moment and felt so dizzy that she had to close her eyes for the last bit.

Alice had a secret. Sometimes—not often, but sometimes—she closed her eyes when she changed lanes on the highway. Not looking gave her a feeling of being immortal. That if her eyes were closed, she was in control of what happens. She had never told this to anyone. It was utterly appalling. She understood that. But maybe she had always lived her life by turning a blind eye. If she closed her eyes there wasn't any evil. Only her intellect. Intellect was a world that was completely under her control. And control was safe.

Once up on the roof, she opened her eyes and walked across black tar that felt soft as a thick carpet.

Blissfully unaware that, at that same moment, the window to the apartment slid shut and locked her out.

She stood at the other end of the building and took a big gulp of wine, while she stared up at the Empire State Building and at the Chrysler Building's Art Deco spire. A shining silver pine cone. But why build such tall buildings? It seemed to her utterly absurd and decidedly arrogant to build buildings that scraped the sky. How could human beings continue to be human in this environment? Still, there was something perversely exciting about it all.

She drank more wine, and noticed that she was trembling all over. Tried to pull herself together—thought pragmatically that it was the result of yesterday's shock and the surrealism of suddenly being near her daughter and, on top of everything, this city. Her elbows on the concrete railing that lined the roof, she looked around.

Alice from Äppelviken was gone. Who was she now—this woman on the roof? She didn't actually know. And that was the first really fun feeling that had surfaced inside her in a very long time. Like tiny butterflies fluttering in her stomach. Not unlike how the fetus had felt in her womb a long time ago. But this was no new life—just a completely new feeling, a wondrous sense of expectation.

* * *

While Alice was standing on the roof feeling euphoric, Babylonia and Gabor hurried into a small theater in the West Village.

And just around the corner of the roof where Alice stood, inside a Chinese dive at Chatham Square, sits Charles—the man with the cigarette, the veined hands and the face framed by long sideburns.

He will soon enter into this story. Thus far, he is still living his own life. For a long time now, he has undoubtedly been breathing the same air as Babylonia and Gabor, has been walking the same streets, perhaps even shopped in the same store at the same time. In a big city people live their own lives without ever noticing one another—until they're pushed together by pure chance. But so far he has only brushed against our story, like a phantom on the periphery.

While Alice stands on the roof completely unaware that she is locked out, Charles—alone as usual—is just finishing a simple meal of fried shrimp dumplings, sesame noodles and spare ribs marinated in hoisin sauce.

He wipes a bit of sauce from the corner of his mouth. Gets up. He is out of tobacco so he buys a pack of Winstons at the cash register by the door.

Out on the street, he lights a cigarette and takes a drag with a sense of deep satisfaction. And then he goes for a little stroll down towards the dark and seedy neighborhood by the East River.

* * *

Alice walked around on the roof and looked at the view. In one direction lay Midtown with its skyscrapers, in the other Wall Street. Chinatown was like a valley between skyscraper mountains. A thought that was followed by immediate euphoria over the fact that even though it was nighttime, and September, it felt like a warm summer evening.

And it smelled. Smelled of exhaust fumes, garbage, people.

This should have disgusted her, but instead she felt almost intoxicated by the scent and the sounds: the constant noise from the air conditioners that hung like big bulky boxes outside apartment windows; police sirens; the aroma of nine million people's sweaty bodies drenched in perfume, secreting garlic, intestinal gases. The stench of rats, cat pee and the licorice-like scent from billions of cockroaches found in everything: in the walls, in the streets, in the ceilings, in the kitchen cupboards; and some mornings even on toothbrushes.

But of that Alice was unaware—so far.

She stood there on the roof and drank the last drops of wine, then returned to the fire escape and began to make her way down to the apartment, eyes closed, holding on tightly to the rails. Thought about having another glass of wine. Why not? She almost never gave herself permission to do something a bit risqué. And truth be told—how risqué was it for a forty-eight year old woman to drink a glass of wine on a roof in New York?

From inside the apartment, Elvis the cat stared at her through the closed window. She tried pulling the window up. But it was stuck. Locked. Impossible to open.

The cat looked almost human, a little triumphant that he was inside and she was outside—locked out. She pulled at the window again. But it didn't budge. With a nervous giggle, she sat down on the edge of the fire escape. Behind her, the cat licked his right paw contentedly. His raspy tongue slid fastidiously between his elegant claws.

And the city continued to move around them.

* * *

At the exact same moment, Göran sat on the couch in the house in Äppelviken and read the note that he'd found in the bedroom. He leaned back, crying a little, took a hefty gulp of the whiskey, walked over to a shelf and opened a large address book. He picked up the phone, dialed a long number.

And in New York, Alice heard the phone ring inside the apartment. She jerked frantically at the window. But it remained locked. Locked solid.

She looked down at the street where a Chinese couple stood bent over the open hood of a blue car. The girl's black hair was gathered in a long ponytail. She was wearing a short white skirt and had long slender legs that looked bare in a pair of thin canvas shoes. The guy wore a red cap, backwards. Their heads were close together hanging over the engine.

Maybe they could help her. She couldn't just sit here on a fire escape outside a window like a fool. In her fine beige suit. For hours. It was strange that no one had noticed her. No one looked at her from any other window. *No one* on the street had noticed that a middle-aged Swedish woman in a beige business suit from the NK Designer Fashion department sat on a filthy fire escape desperately trying to open a closed window.

Carefully, she climbed down the fire escape. It ended a whole floor before street level. She sat on the edge but didn't dare jump. Still felt a bit empowered by the wine. Different. Not like her usual self: an ordinary woman from Äppelviken who had just locked herself out. No, now she was someone else, a person who sits on a rickety iron ladder outside a window in an American city slum.

Or not.

No, things like this didn't happen. Not to her.

But she couldn't just sit there. Couldn't close her eyes and make it all go away. This was really happening.

She was sitting right here. On a rickety fire escape. Locked out.

She gathered her courage.

Thought she raised her voice.

"Hey," she called to the couple. "Hello down there."

But they didn't hear her, continued poking around the engine. He with a screwdriver, while the girl held a small flashlight.

"Hey," she tried again. Now louder. Shriller. She formed a funnel with her hands so that her voice would carry farther.

"Hey. Do you speak English?"

The Chinese man looked up at Alice on the fire escape in surprise and answered her in perfect American English. "Hey. Is everything okay?"

She shook her head.

"Need some help lady?"

He and the girl took a few steps closer so that they stood directly beneath her. Alice crossed her legs. Didn't want them to see up her skirt.

They looked up at her and waited in silence for an explanation.

In faltering Oxford English, she tried to explain about the window that had slammed shut and her daughter who was at the theater. Caught up in her pedantic need to use correct grammar and pronunciation, coherent speech became very difficult to formulate.

The couple looked at each other. The man said something to the girl in Chinese and she went to the trunk of the car and took out a small fold-up ladder. He stepped up on it and stretched his arms up towards Alice.

"Come on, don't be afraid. I'll catch you."

She looked around. She couldn't possibly jump down two meters into a strange Chinese man's arms. But what had she expected? What was she thinking when she'd called to them? Hadn't thought clearly at all. Just yelled down.

The Chinese man nodded encouragingly and held up his arms toward her. The girl smiled kindly, albeit with a bit too much curiosity.

As if in a dream, as if she were in someone else's body, she slipped clumsily over the edge and let herself fall into his arms.

The ladder fell over. They rolled around in the gutter and everything suddenly switched to slow motion as she lay in the dirt—on the street—with the Chinese man's arm around her.

The girl giggled politely, her hand over her mouth. The young man stood up and helped Alice back to her feet.

The girl brushed off her suit, circling around her as if she were an object, a child.

"Are you okay? Anything broken?" the man asked.

Alice looked down at her torn pantyhose. Other than that,

everything felt intact—and they'd managed to brush off most of the dirt.

He held out his hand.

"My name is Henry and this is my fiancée Li Ming."

Li Ming giggled, her hand over her mouth again. Alice shook both their hands gravely. Formally.

"Pleased to make your acquaintance. My name is Alice. And thank you very much again." She swallowed and swallowed. Everything was so strange. And she was so tired. So tired, so tired, so tired.

"No problem..." He fidgeted. "Swedish?" he said suddenly.

"Yes... is it that obvious...?" she stammered.

Henry smiled and switched to fluent Swedish with soft guttural "r" sounds. Chinese speakers often had a hard time pronouncing these but all of Henry "r's" were in a beautiful Småland dialect.

"Me too," he said. "Though not Li Ming, she's from Taiwan. But I'm from Kalmar. Henry Andersson-Chu."

Somewhat rattled, Alice shook hands with him again.

"You're Swedish?"

He nodded and she now saw that he had on a "Torsås' Municipality" T-shirt. She stared at the T-shirt and at his face and suddenly felt drained.

Nothing was logical—everything was confusing. She longed to be back in her familiar world in Äppelviken right now—for the magical city to be just a dream and for her to be sitting in her comfortable beige sofa wrapped in her light yellow robe, holding a cup of tea in her hand, the big blue English cup with the pink flower. Sitting there having no other thoughts about her husband than that he was a little dull—and wondering if he would remember to pick up the dry cleaning on his way home. Everyday life. The usual. Knowing that he would make love to her routinely once a week and that she would sometimes wish him to come quickly so that she could finish the chapter in the book she was reading. All this she longed for. She didn't want to be here. Where Chinese men were from Kalmar, rooftops were soft and cats could lock windows.

She was so tired. And somewhere deep inside she remembered the grief. She had almost suppressed the reason it lay under her skin, burning. That everyday life would never be the same again: that she was forty-eight years old and no longer lived in a reality that felt familiar.

Henry nodded toward the car.

"Well… good night then and hope you have a nice evening. I have to finish up here."

He leaned down over the engine but looked up again when he saw that Alice was still standing there. He looked at Li Ming, and then back at Alice.

"Are you completely locked out? Don't you have a key?"

Alice shook her head and began to wonder why she had made her way down to the street. She could have remained there on the cushion outside the window. Maybe fallen asleep. No matter how absurd that would have been. Instead, she stood here now and was just as locked out as before but with nowhere to sit, no money, no phone numbers, no friends. Had the key to nothing in this horrid, dirty, crazy nightmare.

"Is there no one at home at your daughter's?" Henry continued, quiet and concerned.

"No." And she could hear that she sounded annoyed, looked around. There wasn't a bench in sight. Nothing. And her pantyhose were torn.

"Maybe you can take a taxi to that theater," he said hesitantly.

"I don't know where it is or even what it's called…"

He stood there, silent and pensive.

She wanted so much to explain. If she could only express herself clearly, perhaps everything around her would become less confused. "I just arrived, today, from Sweden," she said.

"I understand," Henry said and looked at Li Ming again. Hesitated.

"I'd really like to help you, but my car broke down."

He nodded toward Li Ming who kept smiling, smiled constantly except when she burst into giggles with her hand over her mouth.

"Her father is on his way to pick us up. Unfortunately, we're in a bit of a hurry."

He continued to look at Alice, worried. "You have no money on you, do you?"

"Money?" Alice said. "No. None at all."

Henry took out his wallet. "Here. You can borrow ten dollars. We Swedes have to stick together. I'm sure you would have done the same for me, right?"

Alice nodded, not at all sure she would have. Simply hand over money to a stranger with no further ado! No, she wouldn't have done that.

He pointed to a fabric store across the street. "I work there. You can pay me back tomorrow."

Hesitantly, she accepted the ten dollar bill. "That's very kind of you." She wanted to say more but didn't get to as a white van came careening down the street and screeched to a halt beside them—in the middle of the street with the motor running. *Mr. Chow's Fish* was painted in big letters on the side of the van. "Come Fly with Me" in Sinatra's seductive caressing voice filled the street. The door to the driver's seat flung open and a small, angry, middle-aged Chinese man jumped out. Completely ignoring Alice, he rushed at Henry and Li Ming, gesticulating wildly and barking incessantly.

Henry took a step back as the man pushed Li Ming aside and forcefully slammed shut the hood of the Ford. With his melodic Mandarin dialect—completely out of sync with Sinatra's song—he hurried Li Ming and Henry Andersson-Chu so that before they even got a chance to stop and say goodbye to Alice, they found themselves sitting next to him in the van, and were immediately whisked away.

Still smiling, Li Ming waved to Alice through the window.

Then they were gone.

And Alice stood alone on the deserted street with a ten dollar bill in her hand.

She looked around. The street was deserted and dark. No nice little cafe where she could sit and wait. They had said that they would be home in just a few hours. She had seen the giant-like man go into the bar a bit further up the street, of course, but it looked like a real dump.

It wasn't cold outside. Maybe she could venture a little walk.

She never had time to react.

It came out of nowhere.

It's impossible, among all the other New York noises, to discern a moped that suddenly pops up behind you.

A small, fragile, dark-haired girl wearing sunglasses was perched behind a hefty guy, her arms around his waist. As they passed Alice, the girl snatched the ten dollar bill from Alice's hand. Alice was so flabbergasted that she didn't even have time to react before the moped was gone.

She stared down at her empty hand, looked around to see if there was anyone who had seen what had happened.

But no one was there.

The street was dark and deserted again.

5

We glide over the city—not too far—and stop just north of Washington Square where the streets are reminiscent of old London with genial small cigar shops, outdoor cafes and pastry shops where you can buy marzipan cakes in the shape of huge erect penises in a variety of pleasant colors. The buildings are covered in ivy and have inviting stoops where you can sit and talk while sharing a joint in the mild autumn evening.

On one of the streets, right next door to one of the erotic bakeries, lay a little basement theater.

Inside, the lobby was now empty and still. Faint music could be heard from inside the theater. But in a narrow toilet that reeked of air freshener, Babylonia sat with her head in her hands.

She didn't have to pee. Just wanted to be alone, felt like she was suffocating. She had seen the show about fifty times now. Wanted so earnestly to find it meaningful. That she was doing meaningful theater. That it would lead to something. But to sit and sell tickets to a mediocre production of *The Taming of the Shrew*, which an idiot of a director had set in 1960s San Francisco, was feeling more and more meaningless.

There were far more actors on stage than audience members in the theater. Everyone worked for free in the hope of being discovered by the odd agent. How could they be discovered in such a lousy production? She never said that out loud. Not even to herself. It was as if everyone pretended that they were actors, pretended that this production was good and meaningful.

Why could nothing in her life ever feel like it was for real? Sure—this toilet was real. The dirty floor she stared at for lack of anything else to look at, the sharp smell of toxic air freshener, all of that was real. But everything else—from her relationship with Gabor to this play—felt as if she was just pretending while she just waited for life to begin. Maybe it would begin next week. But she was twenty-five years old. And she felt more and more that twenty-five was infinitely old. Next year she'd be twenty-six. Before you know it, she'd be thirty and after that it was downhill all the way.

With her head in her hands, she closed her eyes. And when after a while Gabor knocked on the door, she flushed although there was nothing to flush. Wanted it to seem as if she'd peed and wasn't just sitting there. Make-believe routine in everything. What could she do to feel that life was really happening? That it actually was for real.

The lobby was drab and dark. There was a mouse hole in the box office so she avoided sitting there if she didn't have to. Inside the theater "She's Not There" by The Zombies was playing. Thirty minutes left until the play was over, she sighed. Inside the little dark theater, only seven people sat, three of them had comps.

Gabor had gone up to the lighting box again.

Head heavy, as if she were drugged by pure boredom, she stood on tiptoe and looked out the single small window facing the street. Saw feet walking past outside. She decided to lock the door, although it was still possible that someone would come in and buy candy or soda, which Gabor laconically claimed was one of the few sure sources of income for the small theater.

After having locked up properly, she climbed up the stairs to the lighting box and gently pushed the door open. There in the darkness behind the audience, Gabor sat half-asleep over the light board. Down on the stage, 16th century English was being declaimed by people dressed in floral miniskirts and headbands, with peace signs dangling in thick chains around their necks. Gabor looked up as she slid into the booth, took her hand and shushed her.

Petruchio gestured from the stage, past the empty seats and the seven people who sat scattered across the auditorium. With all his soul and maybe a little irony, he cried out, "Worse and worse; she will not come! O vile..." Babylonia liked Petruchio-Brad and smiled down at him as he struggled with the hopeless context and she thought she saw him smile back at her.

She looked down into the audience and saw an elderly man sleeping. The director sat in the back with pen and paper writing feverishly. Someone was in for a reprimand tonight. She leaned back again and sighed. What had she wanted to get out of this? She had wanted to work with theater because it was a world of dreams, illusions. Because it was so clearly fantasy, that it would bring up the madrigals and voices from her childhood. But this? No. She couldn't take *this* seriously. Tomorrow she would quit. Tomorrow she would start something of her own. It should be possible. She could put on her own production.

In the darkness of the theater, everything seemed possible.

Then she remembered that her mother was in town. And she felt completely paralyzed. And angry. Tomorrow, Alice would most certainly point out that her life here was meaningless drivel, that she should give up and come home, maybe enroll at Stockholm University's Department of Behavioral Sciences.

She wished fervently that her mother would just disappear.

Go home.

Not bother her—here.

* * *

Meanwhile, on a corner of Catherine Street amidst all the garbage and odors, Alice stood and peered through the small window of the bar called BAR. The window was high and inaccessible, as if to protect the customers inside from being seen. The only thing she could make out in the gloom was the man at the end of the bar closest to the window.

He turned toward the window: tousled and carelessly cut sandy blond hair. Now she recognized him. Of course, it was the giant she had seen earlier.

When he saw her, he raised an eyebrow, smacked his lips lightly and crooked a long finger at her to come in. A finger that was... gnarled—and several inches long. She flinched and hurried away from the window and on toward Chatham Square up by the Bowery.

Across the street, she saw two brightly lit restaurants, their names displayed on white neon signs with red Chinese characters. Everything looked hostile and alien. What was she doing here, alone in a gray and dirty industrial neighborhood? She wanted to feel clean, warm, safe.

She turned around and walked back toward the apartment. Her whole body felt heavy, tired. How could she have imagined that it was a good idea to travel halfway around the world without having made any arrangements?

Her torn stockings were sticking to her legs. She felt dirty, wanted to shower and brush her teeth. Just one day earlier, she had been a well-groomed university professor in Sweden. How could she have so quickly degenerated into this? Standing here on a strange street with torn stockings, a little drunk. All alone, locked out, with no control over her own destiny. She had nowhere to go and didn't even know where or how to begin to pull herself together.

When she passed the bar again, she stopped. Took a deep breath, smoothed her hair and stepped inside.

The venue was long and narrow, a jukebox stood at the door, a dozen worn bar stools were placed along the brown bar that was made of some unidentifiable type of wood, covered by a sticky film of beer and nicotine.

The giant was now sitting with his back to the door. Despite the high bar stool, his long legs reached the floor. Further into the bar, she could just make out an elderly couple that sat silently in the darkness, each nursing a half-empty glass.

Behind the bar, a dark-haired woman was drying glasses. She was maybe thirty, a bit worn-looking like she just stepped out of a 17th century Dutch painting. Full lips, huge eyes, high cheekbones. The most beautiful woman Alice had ever seen.

When Alice closed the door behind her, the woman looked up from the glass she was wiping with her long slender hands, an old man's hands, hands that looked like they belonged to someone else.

Looking slightly surprised, she put down the glass and her towel. Without really raising her eyebrows, she still looked as if she had. She tilted her head and opened her mouth. "Hi, there. What can I get you, sweetheart?"

Her voice was unusually dark, rasping and sexy, yet melodic.

"Nothing, thank you." Alice went completely silent, aware that she might seem somewhat unsettled. Saw the woman shoot a glance at the giant who was watching with interest.

"Nothing? Really?"

They waited.

Alice felt a need to explain. But explain what exactly? She wanted to turn around and walk out. Regretted that she'd entered in the first place. But remained standing there. Still. Caught in the moment. Stuck standing there in the shabby bar, in this nightmare that was becoming increasingly muddled.

"I'm locked out," she finally said.

"Okay…?"

The giant now had an idiotic smile on his angular face. The woman studied her gravely.

Alice took a step towards the bar and put her hand on the counter. And it was as if she wasn't the one who decided how her body moved, that she was just a marionette controlled by a puppet master.

"Can I just sit here for a little while?"

The woman put her hand over Alice's. It felt damp from the wet dishes.

"Did he throw you out? Or perhaps it was a she…? Poor you. Did you have a fight?"

Alice gently withdrew her hand.

"No, no. She hasn't thrown me out. I don't live here. But they went to the theater. I climbed out on the fire escape and the window closed behind me. I'm locked out. It happened just now… Do you understand…?"

She heard the touch of hysteria in her own voice, but it didn't seem to faze the woman. She looked seriously at Alice.

"In this building?"

The woman lit a cigarette and glanced at the giant. "Which apartment?"

Hadn't they understood what she said? She was having trouble focusing, got stressed out by not being able to make herself understood in a matter so simple, so logical. "No. Not here," she blurted. "At number 120… down the street…"

The beautiful woman continued to study her calmly and kindly with her big dark eyes.

"And you got locked out on the fire escape? Dressed like that. Incredible." She put down the cigarette. "How did you get down?"

The giant suddenly joined in. He leaned forward. Very close. There was something a little crazy in his entire demeanor. "Are you sure that the window is locked? Maybe it's just a very heavy window?"

Alice flinched back from his breath that stank of something indefinable.

"It's locked. Completely locked," she said quickly.

The woman poured a large whiskey, but not in the Swedish way of first measuring the amount of alcohol in exact centiliters. She put the nearly full glass in front of Alice.

"Go ahead. You could use a drink. My treat." She held out her hand. "Amanda from Rotterdam."

Alice took Amanda's hand a little unsure.

"Alice, Sweden."

The giant raised his glass

"Pavel. From Zagreb. Cheers."

And while the night descended over the city, and Babylonia and Gabor could finally lock up the theater, Alice heard herself begin to tell the stranger Amanda about what had happened to her in Sweden. About the man who had been cheating on her with a woman who probably was half her age. Everything came out and her tears began to flow. Amanda stepped out from behind the bar, sat down on the adjacent bar stool and put her arm around her.

Pavel leaned forward and offered Alice a dirty handkerchief that he'd taken out of his pocket. She shook her head. Wounded, he put the handkerchief back in his pocket.

Alice wiped her nose gently on the back of her hand.

"I've lived for twenty-three years with a man I might never have loved—who doesn't love me."

"Things like that can happen to the best of us," comforted Amanda.

Pavel shook his head.

"Monogamy—a lousy idea."

Alice wanted to protest, explain. "But I like monogamy."

"Yeah, yeah... sure. Don't we all." Amanda patted her hand again. "It's just that monogamy is so damn unrealistic... you know."

"No, according to research..." Alice began, but immediately stopped. What was she doing? Oh my God, she must get some sleep soon. And she found herself on the brink of tears again.

"Come on," said Amanda quietly. "Here. Make sure you blow your nose properly now."

Pavel happily offered his handkerchief again. Amanda took it and held it to Alice's nose as if she were a child and forced her to blow into the dirty handkerchief. She had no time to protest before, horrified, she was blowing her clean nose in the filthy handkerchief.

Pavel and Amanda smiled at each other over her head.

* * *

In Sweden, on the other side of the great Atlantic, it was early morning and Göran was trying to stack the dishwasher but dropped a plate on the floor. He tore the entire rack out of the machine. The dishes crashed to the floor and he started screaming like a madman.

"Hell. Shit. Damn it all..."

He fell silent staring at the dishes on the floor, poured himself a large whiskey, sat down on a kitchen stool and downed the contents of the glass.

The clock struck six.

And in New York it was midnight and Göran's wife sat in a beige business suit in a dark, dirty bar on the border between Chinatown and the Lower East Side, staring at an exquisitely beautiful woman who was closing up.

"I'll wait out here on the street. They'll be home soon enough," said Alice uncertainly.

"Oh no. You're coming with us," said Amanda firmly. "We'll show you the real New York. You need to get out and have some fun."

"No, that's alright, thank you. You've been so kind. But they'll be back soon. I'm sure of it..."

Amanda leaned over the bar and put her hand over Alice's. She looked her kindly straight in the eyes with her own large green mesmerizing eyes.

"It's too cold and dangerous to stand out there on the street by yourself. Especially the way you look. We're going to a place nearby. Come with us. We'll take care of you. You need friends like us now."

"Friends like us," echoed Pavel like the vultures in *The Jungle Book.*

And Alice let herself be drawn out into the night.

Amanda locked the door. Pavel helped draw the gates down over the door and windows. And then they secured the gates with a large padlock.

Amanda took Alice's hand and pressed it lightly.

"Come now. Let's go."

Alice was floating on a wave. She couldn't stop anything now. She could only let herself be carried along, with no idea where she was going. She was perhaps a little scared. But also completely stuck in the practical and simple notion of *not* having to take responsibility. Of not being expected to be the one making decisions. Of just walking away with this woman and this burly man along a dirty street full of garbage and the reek of rotting vegetables that had been trashed in front of closed market stalls.

She held Amanda's hand and felt the warmth from this stranger's fingers, realized that she actually hadn't held someone's hand for over fifteen years. Not since her daughter was a child and not since she and her husband first fell in love. But here she was with this hand in hers, feeling a sense of security... and something else—a seed of possibility.

As they disappeared around the corner, a taxi stopped outside number 120. Babylonia and Gabor jumped out, hurried into the building and up the stairs.

They just missed seeing Alice being dragged down through deepest Chinatown, to a more obscure and seedy neighborhood by the East River.

* * *

And now our story is under way.

We take a breath. Feel the fragrances, sense the darkness. Salsa flows relentlessly from dilapidated cars driving by, windows open to let in some air. Roosters crow. Voices, mad with longing for love, heroin or someone who should have been home with a paycheck several hours ago, bounce against the worn walls. The crying of cats in heat is mixed with the barks of fighting dogs tearing each other apart in the yard next door.

And the mother and the daughter's boundaries are dissolving.

Both transformed into the same thing...

Or maybe into something completely different.

We continue.

6

In a brightly lit ping-pong hall on Pitt Street at the foot of the Williamsburg Bridge, two tall, athletic young men were playing ping-pong. They played silently, completely focused on the game. The venue was bare and unattractive. Aside from the sound of the ball bouncing on the table, there was only the faint whir of a ceiling fan, accompanied by the desolate hum of a vending machine.

Leaning against the side of the humming vending machine was a solitary spectator, watching the game. This is Charles, who now enters our story.

In a well-tailored suit with wide trousers and a knitted gray vest, Charles stands there with an empty martini glass in one hand. In the other, he's holding a cigarette. His face is narrow and sad, with long and bushy sideburns, the kind that are more appropriate on a man in a 19th century novel. In fact, nothing about him belonged in this bleak ping-pong hall with its stark white fluorescent lighting.

Alice didn't notice the man standing there with a martini glass in hand, watching her closely as Amanda led the way through the place.

On their walk here through the increasingly dark and shabby streets, she had felt as if she were gliding through a landscape on the border between dreams and reality. That the goal of the walk turned out to be a fluorescent-lit ping-pong hall seemed so absurd that she found herself accepting it unquestioningly. Why wouldn't they wind up here watching a ping-pong match under fluorescent lights in the middle of the night?

Amanda grabbed the handle to a trapdoor. She turned to Alice and took her hand. Alice peered through the opening in the floor and saw worn stone steps leading down to a dark basement. The smell of cigars and cigarette smoke wafted up. You could hear jazz music intermingled with the faint murmur of voices.

"Come on, it's a bit steep, but hold my hand and you'll be okay."

Pavel followed close behind and closed the door above them.

Had Alice been in her right mind, she might not have followed two strangers down a steep staircase into a dark cellar that smelled of sweet smoke, men's perfume and booze. However, over the past hour, life had increasingly begun to seem like an alcohol-induced dream and dreams aren't necessarily logical. So Alice could only note objectively that this was obviously some sort of party venue.

When her eyes had adjusted to the dark, she noticed that the place was full of people who were milling around in the dimness. Miles Davis was playing from the discreetly placed speakers, and ghostlike people were smoking and drinking on couches in the dark corners of the room. From what she could tell, the clientele varied in age, many of them wearing suits or cocktail dresses.

"But why are they playing ping-pong up there?" she asked while Amanda navigated her way among the guests toward a dimly lit bar where a lone bartender stood and jiggled a cocktail shaker.

"So that no one will know the club is down here, darling," Amanda said.

"But if no one knows there's a club here, no one will find it."

"Those who should find it, will find it."

Alice had never liked ambiguity and liked it even less here in the hazy room that was unlike any place she had ever been.

"But why play ping-pong? Why not just stand there and guard the entrance?" she persisted, and heard herself slur the consonants in the word ping-pong.

"They play so that no one..." Amanda paused, stopped and squeezed her hand. "Don't worry about it. I'll buy you a drink, love. White wine okay?" She waved at the bartender.

"I like it when things are what they appear to be," Alice said, this time carefully and clearly.

"Me too, darling."

Amanda placed a plastic cup filled with wine in Alice's hand and patted her gently on the arm as if she were a tiresome child, all the while pushing her ahead toward three gentlemen dressed in suits who sat in red plush armchairs smoking cigars.

She sat down on the arm of one of the chairs, bent over a man with silver hair and kissed him softly on both cheeks. With her head near his mouth, she listened to something he whispered in her ear. She threw back her head in a wide open laugh so casually elegant in her thin black silk coat, a coat Alice had thought was a strange choice of clothing for the shabby bar called BAR. But here in the underworld, Amanda and her black silk coat fit in perfectly. Alice stood next to her, the plastic cup in her hand, dressed in her practical thin wool suit. It had been quite right for the flight but here it made her feel uncomfortable and out of place.

A magnificent couple had just started a tango-like dance to the soft music and it was as if she was surrounded by a mist of the sweet, herbal-smelling cigarette smoke that she'd noticed when they opened the cellar door.

She smelled the wine. It smelled sour and the plastic cup looked dirty. She wished she had a Perrier—plain old mineral water. Even regular Swedish tap water would be wonderful. Not sour, white wine in a plastic cup in an underground room that branched out into dark nooks that seemed like infinite darkness.

Amanda pushed her slightly and nodded toward a dark-skinned man dressed in a tuxedo sitting on one of the sofas. He raised his glass and winked at Alice and gestured toward the empty space beside him. Amanda nodded encouragingly but Alice turned away. Oh my God. What was she doing here? Enough was enough. She wasn't going to sit next to him, wasn't going to drink anymore wine. Felt a huge wave of determination taking hold of her again. She had to go back to the apartment on Catherine Street NOW and wait for them to come home.

But she didn't move. Was unable to move, as if an invisible rope held her in place. As if she was in an intricate endless nightmare, in a web of confusing events that were woven around her.

* * *

Back at the apartment, Babylonia hurried through the bedroom and stopped at the door to the front room. No one had made up the couch.

Elvis sat like a king on the pile of folded sheets and stared at them with that drowsy and triumphant look that cats have when they've gotten the upper hand.

"Where could she have gone?"

Alice's suitcase stood unopened at the foot of the sofa, her handbag neatly on the floor next to it.

"There's no note. My mother always leaves a note."

Gabor pushed the cat away and sat down on the couch next to the sheets. Elvis stalked towards the bookshelf, tail held high, insulted. Showed as clearly as he could how much he disliked everything about the burly Hungarian.

Gabor took her hand as she stared down at her mother's bags.

"Don't worry. Maybe she went out for a walk. Maybe she's at the bar on the corner. That wouldn't be so strange."

Babylonia opened the window.

"My mother doesn't go into bars." She stuck her head out and looked towards the bar. "And, anyway, it looks closed."

She sat on the window sill and looked around the room. "And another thing...she doesn't have any keys. She couldn't have gone out. The door was locked."

She remembered a "game" they had played when she was little, where her mother had pretended to disappear. Maybe she wanted to study her reaction. Babylonia had rushed around, terrified, thinking herself alone in a gigantic department store filled with green lampshades, among strange legs and rugs with horrible, indecipherable patterns, while Alice watched her from a distance.

Or maybe that's not what had happened at all. Maybe her mother really had lost her. And concealed her own fear when she finally found her by calling what had happened a game.

Now the adult Babylonia sat there at the window and felt equally lost. Could she be absolutely certain that Alice wouldn't just pop up like a jack-in-the-box from a closet, smiling, friendly?

Gabor leaned out the window beside her. The smell of marijuana from the neighbors' open window wafted in, a soft puff through the night air.

And then they saw it. An empty wine glass stood beside the cushions on the fire escape. A few red drops were left in the bottom of the glass.

She picked up the glass and sniffed it.

"Red wine," she noted. "Strange. A glass... here."

Gabor looked at the wine glass and then up toward the roof. Babylonia followed his gaze and crawled out onto the fire escape. Don't be afraid. She's there. Up there.

The phone rang inside the room. He turned around and walked over to the bookshelf, picked up the phone. Held his hand over the receiver and whispered.

"Your father. He sounds quite drunk. Isn't it morning in Sweden now?"

7

Some of the men stood up, leaving room to sit on one of the sofas. Amanda pulled Alice down beside her.

"How are you feeling now, love?" Amanda rolled a thin cigarette, smiled and waved to someone who passed by in the dark. "Isn't this place great?" she whispered.

Soft voices buzzed around them, the music was mellow and sad. A young girl in a shimmering green dress, who looked no older than sixteen or seventeen, danced by herself near the stairs that led to the trapdoor above.

"Forget him now—your husband. Life can be whatever you want it to be. Trust your friend Amanda. I know, you know."

She blew out smoke and Alice turned away to avoid breathing it in. "So, answer the question. Don't you like it here?" she repeated, her voice thick from the smoke she'd just inhaled. "No tourists or bridge and tunnel types find their way here. You get it, right?"

"It's very dark in here," was the only response Alice could manage. And what could she say? Maybe as a young student she would have thought it was exciting to sit in an underground club drinking alcohol. Now it just felt impractical. But would Amanda understand that? That if she were to have a drink at all, she'd prefer to have it in a nice hotel bar. With a view. And that to drink while the night was about to turn into dawn felt like something she had put behind her before she'd even begun acquiring such habits.

Someone tapped her on the shoulder. With a nod toward the dark-skinned man wearing a tuxedo, a bartender in a suit handed her an empty plastic cup. He filled the cup with whiskey. The man nodded at her and raised his own glass. She put down the wine that Amanda had given her and stared into the cup of whiskey. It was all incomprehensible. What was she, Alice, doing here? No, this whole adventure had to come to an end. She looked at the time, leaned forward and patted Amanda's hand.

"I think I'll go home now."

Amanda waved her hand dismissively. Intent on what one of the men was saying, she took Alice's hand in her own and held it.

Alice tried again.

"Which way do I walk to get back to Catherine Street?"

Amanda turned to Alice, a pointed look in her green eyes.

"We just got here. Stay a while. I promise I'll take you home later." She stood up. "Wait here, I'll be right back. Talk to Sal. He owns Cucina Carmela."

She patted Alice on the shoulder, as if everyone knew what Cucina Carmela was. Then she disappeared into the crowd.

Sal, a well-dressed, gracious man in his fifties smiled politely at Alice. He had a friendly smile beneath a pair of cold reptilian eyes, thick lips and a somewhat impatient demeanor. She smiled back but then looked away. Had neither the energy nor the inclination to waste her Oxford English on him. Out of the corner of her eye, she watched him beckon to a woman in her twenties. The girl, who was unnaturally busty for her frail body, came over and sat on his lap. Her shiny dress was so low cut that most of her chubby breasts were exposed, except for the nipples.

The man who'd sent over the whiskey was gone. The girl who'd been dancing by herself near the stairs was now staring at Alice. When she saw Alice looking in her direction, she came over and plunked herself down on the sofa where Amanda had just been sitting. Her shimmering green silk dress hugged her skinny teenage body. She crossed her long legs, smiled and pinched the fabric of Alice's suit jacket. She held the fabric and caressed it with her hand. Her hands were rough and manly with long, slender fingers, the nails pale pink. Her voice had an astonishing bass tone. A sorrowful heaviness.

"Such a beautiful jacket. Such fine fabric. Agnès b, right?"

"Alice Berglund," replied Alice and quickly realized that she'd said something wrong.

The girl, who perhaps was a boy, looked confused and asked, "Who's that?"

She didn't answer, but stood up, looked around—and had no idea where to go.

* * *

And back at the apartment, Babylonia sat looking out the window with a cup of tea in her hand. The cats' eyes glowed in the dark. Gabor was in bed snoring, the sound mixing with the incessant police sirens and the whirring of air conditioners from the neighboring buildings.

Across the way, some women were already busy at their sewing machines, toiling in that fuzzy boundary between night and day.

Several blocks away, down by the East River, something went off, sounding like a gunshot, or a car exhaust. Or maybe it was just an ordinary firecracker.

But the neighbor's rooster was still quiet. Because despite the fact that for the women in the sweatshop the workday was endless, night still enveloped the city.

* * *

Alice took a few steps, looked around—but Amanda and Pavel were nowhere to be found. Cigarette smoke lay like a filter between her and the gray shapeless shadows that milled around and sometimes bumped into her as if they didn't see her. As if she weren't there, was invisible, someone who was out of place standing there looking around in her suit from NK Ladies Fashion. How could they just have abandoned her? What would happen if a fire broke out in this place? Would she be able to open the trapdoor above the steep stone steps by herself? Perhaps it would be best simply to relax and just wait to wake up? If everything was a dream—then she would wake up if a fire started. But could you really feel drunk if you were in your own dream?

She looked around and there, through the shadow-like creatures milling around, she finally recognized Pavel. Like a lighthouse in the fog, she thought gratefully. He swayed a little, and smiled his slightly idiotic smile.

"Where do you think you're going?"

"I'm very tired," she replied, relieved that he was standing in front of her. "I'll try to make my way back to my daughter's apartment. Can you just help me up to the street?"

Pavel put his hand on her shoulder. "But you don't have any money."

"I don't need money," she said quickly. "I'll walk. It wasn't that far." She removed his hand, but he put his arm around her instead, and looked down at her gravely.

"Someone like you can't go walking around this neighborhood without an escort. Even you must realize that."

His arm around her shoulders felt uncomfortably intimate. She tried to pull away but he held her tightly, close, and she smelled the odor of thousands of cigarettes from his jacket. She tried not to breathe through her nose, but standing there with her mouth open made her feel like she was gasping for air. She closed her eyes for a few seconds to suppress the panic, took a deep breath and mumbled, "Why not? Just point me in the right direction."

Pavel interrupted her, leading her toward a curtain farther back in the room.

"It's too dangerous for you to walk out there alone, darling. Listen to Pavel now, he knows." He smiled and in the dim lighting, it looked like he was missing several teeth in the back of his mouth.

"Just do me one favor," he continued, "and I'll fix you up with taxi money."

Pavel kept a tight grip on her shoulders and pulled her through the curtain. Behind it was a hidden door.

He knocked lightly—a rhythmic knock that sounded like a signal. Someone peered at them through the peephole and then slid the door open and they were admitted.

A man in a black suit raised his eyebrows when he saw Alice, cast a questioning look in Pavel's direction. Pavel nodded and shook his hand. She suspected that money had changed hands, but couldn't be sure.

A roulette table stood in the middle of the room. Three men were playing in silence while an equally silent croupier spun the wheel. Everything was grave and still, everything except the roulette ball bouncing around in its brown wooden bowl bordered with numbers in green and red. When the ball stopped at a number, the men looked down quietly while the dealer cleared the table.

Next to the roulette table, at another game table, a lone woman wearing a burgundy swimsuit with a small rabbit tail and black fishnet stockings shuffled a deck of cards, an absent veiled expression in her dark eyes. She didn't even look up when Alice and Pavel slipped through the door.

Pavel pulled Alice to the roulette table. Silently, they stood for a while, watching the game. He was behind her with his arm on her shoulder. The bouncing ball had an almost hypnotic effect. After a while, he bent forward and whispered in her ear.

"You look like you have beginner's luck. I myself am not trusted, you understand..."

She turned around in dismay. "But I can't..."

He looked down at her, serious, quiet. Looked into her eyes. She hadn't noticed that his eyes were so black, despite his blond hair. She felt dizzy.

"Hey, it's going to be okay," he said softly touching her lightly on the cheek, and like magic, he suddenly had a five dollar bill in his hand.

"Go ahead." He leaned forward. "It's easy."

"But..." was all she got out before he turned her around toward the table as if she were a doll.

"Try number 16," he whispered. "I'll be standing over there." He retreated into the shadows by the wall.

She had never played roulette before, she just wanted to go home and at first stood still with the five dollar bill in her hand. Felt that she had to pee. She turned and met Pavel's gaze. He nodded gravely toward the table and, as if hypnotized, she put the five dollars down. The dealer took the bill and without looking up at her, slid over a couple of chips.

First, she placed just one chip on number 16. When the ball immediately landed on 16, she wasn't even surprised. Nothing could surprise her anymore tonight. Here she stood in her beige suit in a secret underground room under a bridge in downtown Manhattan playing roulette. Everything was perfectly normal and she won again and again.

* * *

Babylonia wanted to sleep. But how could she when her mother was locked out, wandering around out there alone in the city. She sat down on the cushion on the fire escape, leaned her head against the wall and looked down at the bar called BAR, as if she could will the door open with her eyes and find her mother in there in the dark.

One of the city's sanitation trucks drove slowly down the street. It left round water rings behind it, but most of the trash remained, shoved a little to the side by the truck's brushes.

Her eyes met the gaze of one of the seamstresses across the street. The woman's face was expressionless. Hostile. Empty. She lowered her head over the machine and continued to work on the garment she was sewing.

Babylonia crawled back into the apartment and closed the window to shut out the noise. Went to bed where Gabor was fast asleep on his back with his head facing the wall. She sat on the edge of the bed and nudged him.

Gabor sighed and turned his head. Sat up sleepily. "Okay. You want us to go out and look for her, right?"

She took his hand. "What do you think we should do?"

"If your mother locked herself out, she would have made her way to a coffee shop or some hotel, don't you think?" He lay down again. "She got herself here on her own and isn't handicapped, right?"

"True, but she doesn't even have her handbag."

He grabbed his pack of cigarettes, empty. A sigh.

"I never carry a handbag."

"Don't be silly... but on the other hand, Mom would undoubtedly have gotten a hotel room without her wallet. She never takes "no" for an answer. She's the type who would ask the mailman to change a light bulb for her in the middle of his postal route—as if she doesn't understand that people have other things to do. You know what I mean?"

"Sounds pretty normal," he yawned.

"Not the way she does it." She nudged him harder. "Can't you go down look for her? I'll stay here in case she calls."

He didn't make a move.

"Please. Don't tell me that you're tired," she hissed. "How can you be tired? You never do anything."

He pushed her aside and stood up. Now noticeably irritated, he pulled on a pair of jeans that lay on the floor by the bed not bothering with underwear.

"One minute you're leaving me and the next you want me to care about your mother. What is it you really want? You're so heartless."

She patted him on the arm.

"Don't get so upset."

He stood rigid and mad, with his pants unbuttoned, his fly open, naked underneath. She caught a glimpse of his black pubic hair.

He leaned forward and wanted to kiss her. Caressed her breasts gently. She grabbed his hand, held on to it tightly and leaned her head against his shoulder. And then they just stood there, in the little room, beneath the poster with the enormous 50-foot woman—and relaxed in their intimacy.

* * *

Stacks of gambling chips now lay in front of Alice. With his mouth close to her ear, Pavel whispered, "Nice work. I think it's time to cash in..."

He nodded to the dealer, who exchanged the chips for a thick wad of banknotes without uttering a word.

Pavel smacked his lips. "Good girl. I knew it..." But then he stiffened and looked around like an animal that, smelling danger, sniffed the air.

Two men, dressed in well-tailored suits that fit snugly across their broad shoulders and muscular upper arms, had detached themselves from the shadows of the arch against the wall.

Pavel leaned in to Alice's ear again.

"I'll be right back. Wait here."

Alice looked around, confused.

But he'd disappeared into the crowd.

Simply gone.

The room was dim. And it was hard to make anything out in the darkness. She'd been having problems with her night vision for a few years now. Shadows, faces, movements flowed together, contours became blurred. She gathered up her pile of bills. Had no purse to put the money in and her suit pockets weren't designed to store bundles of cash. Could she just walk around with a wad of cash in her hand?

She didn't notice him approaching. Suddenly she felt a hand quietly upon her own. She stared at the big hairy hand, raised her eyes and met the smile of a well-dressed man with a prominent moustache. He stood much too close, distinct in his proximity. His eyes weren't in the least bit friendly, despite the smile.

She took a step backwards.

His mouth was approaching her ear. "Maybe I should introduce myself. The name is Barry."

He nodded down to the money.

"The thing is, we play just for fun. The money stays here."

Alice looked down at her pile of money.

"But that can't be right."

She looked around. "I won this money for Pavel."

"Pavel?" Barry raised his eyebrows, amused. "Who is Pavel?"

She tried to see the logic in him not knowing who Pavel was. He had been there only a short while ago. She looked the man straight in the eye and explained succinctly and clearly. "He was here just now. I didn't want to play roulette. *He* wanted me to. I wanted to go home."

Barry just stared at her with his hairy hand firmly over hers and the money.

"He'll be back soon," she continued. "I'm from Sweden. Alice Berglund is my name."

He leaned even closer to her. She could smell his cigar breath.

"Barry Whinestine. And don't you worry, little lady. Leave the money here, and I'll buy you a drink at the bar out there. I'll even arrange for our chauffeur to drive you home."

Alice felt completely stymied by what he said, felt the room was closing in on her, that what this guy Barry said was actually totally wrong—that what was happening to her right now wasn't quite right.

"Listen here. I won this money legitimately."

He took her by the arm.

"This way, lady."

Instinctively, she grabbed hold of her bundle of cash. They couldn't do this. Not even here.

Barry nodded to one of his broad-shouldered colleagues who calmly glided forward to them.

At the same time, another man emerged from the shadows of the far wall.

Charles, the man who we saw earlier standing upstairs at the ping-pong table pondering his martini, now steps into our story. He sets his glass down on a shelf by the wall and takes a step forward towards the woman who is so obviously in the wrong place, at the wrong time.

Charles gently took Alice by the elbow, removed the money from her hand and put it on the table.

"I think it's best that you listen to them," he whispered. "Come with me. I'll help you get a cab."

He turned to Barry and said loudly, "This lady is a good friend of mine. She's never been here before. I'll take care of this."

She looked up at him, confused but relieved. Felt so incredibly tired.

"Thank you," she said simply.

He took her arm.

"This way, my dear."

Cigar smoke enveloped the nightclub and neither Amanda nor Pavel were anywhere to be found. Two young women sat on Sal's lap now. Another man at the table was laying out lines of white powder on a mirror. A rolled up dollar bill was circulating the table.

"What is this place, anyway?" Alice asked as Charles led her toward the stone stairs.

He smiled and took her elbow as he led her up the stairs.

"What is someone like YOU doing in a place like this?" He shook his head. "That's what I'd like to know."

He held the trapdoor open and offered her his hand as she climbed the final steps. Alice turned and looked down at the closed trapdoor.

"What if a fire started? No one would be able to get out. This would never be allowed in Sweden."

"Not here either," replied Charles dryly and politely opened the door to the street for her. The ping-pong players played on. The trapdoor was no longer visible.

If you didn't know it was there.

* * *

Babylonia lifted the receiver again to check that the phone wasn't dead, but the dial tone indicated that everything was fine. Nothing wrong with the phone. The only thing that was wrong was that her mother had appeared from Sweden and then just disappeared. Evaporated, like a ghost. If the suitcase from Palmgren wasn't standing there by the vinyl couch as incontrovertible evidence that she really had been there, Alice's arrival could be part of a strange dream.

Gabor walked towards the door. "Okay. I'll take a look around the neighborhood. She's probably at an all-night coffee shop nearby."

"Mugged."

"Without her purse she can't be mugged."

"True."

He patted her on the head. "Don't worry. The phone will ring as soon as I leave. I'm sure she'll be sitting here when I get back."

He put his hand on his stomach and grimaced so she would show a little sympathy. But she looked demonstratively away. Couldn't deal with him too.

* * *

Alice felt it was perfectly normal—under the circumstances—that a yellow taxi stopped outside the premises at the exact same moment that they stepped out onto the street. Charles opened the back door and Alice climbed in.

He held out his hand.

"Charles," he said.

His hand was unexpectedly cold and dry.

"Alice," she said simply but withheld her last name for now. It didn't feel important as she sat on the worn burgundy backseat of the taxi with this odd stranger.

She gave the driver Babylonia's address and they leaned back.

Charles took out a pack of cigarettes but didn't light one. He just fiddled with it while he studied her from the other end of the seat.

"So you say you're from Sweden?" He smiled. "I should have guessed. Really outrageous to find a lady like you at that club."

She didn't answer, thought it was odd that a man who looked like this man even existed. He looked like a person in a play, like a cartoon character. She couldn't help but wonder if his long sideburns were genuine or glued on.

He cocked his head to one side. "But, do you really want to go home already, my dear?"

His eyes opened wide and his nostrils expanded so that he now looked even more like a cartoon character, if that were even possible. "Can't I buy you a cup of coffee? There's a nice all-night coffee shop not far from your place."

"I really don't know..."

"It's a nice coffee shop," he continued good-naturedly not taking notice of what she said. "Not at all seedy like some of those places can be. They usually already have the morning edition of *The New York Times* at this hour."

"I'm too tired, but thanks anyway. I got locked out," she explained slowly and clearly so that he would understand. "My daughter should be back by now."

He winked at her as if he were sharing an incredible secret. "They have absolutely amazing raspberry muffins at this coffee shop, I promise you."

She fidgeted.

"I have to call my daughter. Got locked out like I said..."

"Don't worry. There's a payphone at my coffee shop."

He knocked on the taxi partition, and turned simultaneously toward Alice with a friendly smile.

"I'm not the type to force anyone. But it would be very nice to have a chat with someone from Sweden."

He gave the taxi driver a new address.

Alice closed her eyes and once again felt like she was floating or falling—falling through a big black hole into a bottomless new world, a disorganized world with no plans, where her own strong will hung fluttering. Unanchored.

* * *

Babylonia had fallen asleep on the couch. Elvis played on the floor. The telephone receiver that he'd managed to knock off now lay beside the phone. The rug was scrunched up.

From his vantage point on top of the bookcase, Loser was looking at him with disgust. Inside the wall next to him, a cockroach colony was establishing itself. His tail swung slowly. His keen sensory organs felt the presence of the creepy creatures, so brazenly close. Just behind the thin wall.

Elvis noted the other cat's tail wagging, lay on the floor beside the discarded receiver—and waited. The cockroaches sensed the cats and stopped their march.

And Babylonia slept on—unaware of everything that was happening around her.

* * *

Only a few blocks away on Centre Street, just north of Canal, Alice climbed out of the taxi and followed Charles through the open door of an all-night coffee shop.

And a couple of blocks away we find Gabor briskly walking through the dark streets.

He peeked into a couple of all-night bars and coffee shops but decided that the whole thing was idiotic, that finding herself locked out, Alice would certainly have checked into a hotel. He'd continue for a couple more blocks and then turn around and go home.

8

"Nice to see you here so early, Charlie." The man behind the counter immediately handed them a New York Times.

"How's it going, Lewis. Let me introduce my friend Alice."

"Pleased to meet you," replied Lewis pleasantly.

She said hello and looked around. Everything here seemed familiar. More at home than a food establishment in any other foreign country. This was after all a foreign country. On a foreign continent. But hadn't she met the man behind the counter, Lewis, many times before? With her English teacup in hand, at home on the couch in front of the family's Bang & Olufsen TV? Hundreds of versions of him throughout forty years of watching American television series and movies. He was moderately overweight. Looked friendly. Was perhaps of Greek or Italian descent, about fifty-five years old. And here he was—in front of her—and he was for real. Could it be that foreigners visiting Sweden saw Ingmar Bergman's film characters in each dour Swedish academic they met? It was a fun idea and she smiled and Lewis, who thought the smile was for him, smiled back and winked.

Charles took the newspaper from him. "And how's business tonight then?"

"It's very quiet, as you can see," said Lewis. "But I can't complain."

He nodded appreciatively in Alice's direction.

"What a nice looking woman."

"From Europe. Sweden."

"I see. An old acquaintance, perhaps?"

Charles shook his head and turned to Alice. "Hungry, right? Best breakfast in town."

Lewis made a sweeping gesture over the almost empty coffee shop. "Welcome. Sit wherever you'd like. Carole will take care of you. Your usual table just became available."

Everything was as it should be. Orange plastic tables and booths. No tablecloths but clean surfaces everywhere. Further down the counter, two policemen sat with guns carelessly hanging out of holsters, each with a cup of coffee, eating sugary donuts. They licked their fingers and looked with interest at Charles and Alice as they walked by.

He led her to a table by the window and let her choose where she wanted to sit before sitting down himself.

There was something almost old-fashioned about him, a mixture of dusty bachelor and something else. Not something unpleasant or dangerous; but something familiar, though in a different way than the coffee shop and Lewis. As if Charles were one of those authoritative relics who'd been working at the university back home in Stockholm for the past quarter century, delivering the same routine lectures; someone who was about to give up, a person who reeked of the past. And yet he looked no older than she did, maybe even younger. Although his clothes—the gray suit with the knitted vest he wore despite the heat—belonged to a different era.

She liked that he was the antithesis of Göran with his expensive suits and well-ironed shirts. Whatever Charles was, he wasn't a cold, calculating businessman. And maybe it wasn't a dusty university bachelor sitting across the table from her, maybe he was someone out of a yellowed Bloomsbury group photograph. As if he'd stepped straight out of the photo into this strange new reality in which she was a reluctant participant.

He stroked his chin, met her gaze. His eyes were unexpectedly blue.

"Are you hungry?"

She hadn't thought about it until he asked, but now she felt that she was famished.

"Yes, indeed." She smiled.

"Then you have to take a look at their selection of muffins. It's the best in the city."

He opened one of the menus that were wedged between the ketchup and mustard bottles.

A tired waitress in her fifties emerged from the kitchen with a coffee pot. Without being asked, she poured coffee into two cups that had already been set on the table.

"Carole! How are you? You look tired," said Charles amiably.

"My back," she sighed. "But don't worry about me. What can I get you two lovebirds?"

Charles ordered for them both—raspberry muffins, challah bread and scrambled eggs. Alice leaned back in her chair. Normally, it would irritate her that he ordered without asking her first, but at this point she was so tired that it just felt pleasant.

He folded the menus again, and sat back as he picked up his pack of cigarettes.

"You do like eggs? If I ordered too much, you can always take the leftovers home to your daughter. Mind if I smoke?" He took out a cigarette and tapped it against his hand before he lit it. In silence, he then carefully arranged the salt and pepper shakers so that they stood in a straight line with the ketchup and mustard bottles. He placed his coffee cup to his right. Gently, he moved her cup so that it stood in the same place as his own but on her side of the table.

"I like order," he said as if an explanation were needed. "Weren't you going to make a call?"

Alice looked around for a payphone. Charles picked out a few coins from a small old-fashioned purse in black leather and pointed to the payphone.

She sensed the policemen's prying eyes follow her as she walked towards the door where a simple silver metal payphone was hanging on the wall. The receiver was dirty and covered with fingerprints. She held it a good distance from her mouth and ear while she dialed her daughter's number. To her surprise, she got a busy signal. She hung up and went into the restroom to wash her hands before their breakfasts arrived at the table.

* * *

Gabor looked around. No Alice at this coffee shop either. There was only a middle-aged man with bushy sideburns. Two Irish cops sat at the counter. Their pistols hung provocatively loose in their holsters.

Gabor sighed and walked out again. Turned homeward towards Catherine Street.

* * *

She sat down again at Charles's regular table where Carole had just put down two giant muffins, a pile of white challah bread, a saucer with jam and packets of butter and two plates of scrambled eggs.

"No answer?" he asked, and spread butter and jam on her muffin.

"No, I keep getting a busy signal." Warily, Alice broke off a piece of the thick challah bread. "I really don't know what I'm going to do." From the corner of her eye, she saw the policemen nod kindly at her as they got ready to go.

"I guess I have to try and find a hotel," she murmured and put a small piece of bread in her mouth again. But how could she get a hotel room without her wallet? And how could she enter a hotel lobby with torn stockings, without the suitcase from Palmgrens? As if she were a crazy woman?

Charles leaned forward and put down his cutlery at a perfect angle to his plate. "May I make a suggestion?"

He nodded toward the counter where Lewis appeared behind a tray of cakes.

"My friends Lewis and Carole over there behind the counter can vouch for me. I've eaten breakfast here for almost ten years now."

She listened to his suggestion and much to her surprise she heard herself accepting his offer as if it were the most natural thing in the world.

* * *

The receiver was still on the floor. After hanging it up and chasing Elvis out into the kitchen, Gabor woke Babylonia, who'd fallen asleep on the couch clutching her mother's unfolded sheets. He gently undressed her and put her to bed. They lay there awake with their arms entwined around each other while the sun rose over Manhattan.

* * *

Charles unlocked the one simple lock on the door. Alice was surprised that he didn't have as many locks as her daughter had.

"No need in this building," he said. "Little Italy." He winked. "A landlord with connections. You know what I mean?"

She didn't get the link between a landlord in Little Italy and flimsy locks but was too tired to even think about asking him to explain. He pointed to the phone standing on a dresser by the door. She took out the note with Babylonia's number from her pocket again.

Babylonia sat up in bed, suddenly wide awake.

"But, Mom, you can't just sleep over at a complete stranger's..."

"I know Charles," said Alice.

"Dad called... he said you'd had a falling out."

"That may be," Alice said slowly.

"He didn't say why. He also wants to come here now."

"Here?"

"Yes, he said it was a misunderstanding."

"I understand perfectly well."

They fell silent. Neither of them dared to talk about what it was that she understood perfectly. Why she had impulsively hopped on a plane over the Atlantic.

Finally, Babylonia whispered, resigned, "Mom, who is this Charles?"

"He's not dangerous. Completely normal. Almost like a Swede."

"But you can't just... Mom."

Both were silent again.

"Call as soon as you wake up... promise me that," said Babylonia gently.

"Get some sleep, honey," Alice said, and realized that for the first time in her life she would be sleeping in the home of a complete stranger, a man no less.

* * *

But Babylonia wasn't happy about this, as she sat on the bed in the small stuffy apartment on Catherine Street.

Through the door, she could see her mother's unwieldy suitcase in light brown leather on the floor next to the vinyl couch. The handbag with a gold clasp sat beside it.

"We should have told her to come straight home."

"Do you always keep track of what your mother does?"

He tried to pull her down beside him again.

She stared indignantly at him. How could he just calmly lie there? Didn't he know that this didn't even remotely resemble her usual mother? And that it scared her so much that she almost couldn't breathe? As if her childhood nightmares and voices were gnawing at the inside of her skull, creating a dangerous parallel world that had seized hold of her mother and transformed her into something else.

"Did you always keep track of what she was doing in Sweden?" he continued objectively.

"No. When I lived at home, she drove to her office at the university, where she stayed until she got home—then she watched the news, read, and went to bed." Babylonia paused and sighed. "She didn't go out on the town, like this."

"How do you know?" said Gabor. "You haven't lived there in four years. Maybe she's been leading a secret life on campus. She's pretty hot for an old lady."

She crawled into bed and let the familiar scent of his skin envelop her. Gabor was in any case always the same. He certainly didn't change.

"Hardly," she murmured against his chest. "Secret life, I mean. And hot? No, she's totally uninterested in things like that."

"How do you know?"

She turned on her back and looked at the ceiling. "She's only interested in her work, her routines."

"But you're the same. Everything you do is also mostly routine."

"Me?" She turned to him, met his gaze, sharply. "I live here with you in New York and work at a theater. How routine is that?"

"Sounds like everyone else I know."

"What does a person have to do to qualify as interesting to you, then?" she snapped back. "Maybe getting depressed would do it?"

He sighed.

"No, I like you the way you are. Though you might consider picking up a hobby or cultivating some special interests is all I'm saying."

"Me? *You're* the one who does nothing all day."

"I study."

"Film studies! What the hell are you going do with that?"

"What you do with it isn't the point. The point is to grow until you discover what you want. But you just run around. Like a mouse on a treadmill. Stop and focus on something, then you'll become interesting."

She was silent for a few seconds, but then blurted out, "I'm not interesting?"

"I didn't say that."

"We have to stop this. I'm just going to get angry." She was already so angry that she wanted to hit him. He simply didn't know the real her. That was it. "Let's go to sleep," she snapped, slowing her breathing consciously in order to calm down.

"You just don't like hearing the truth. You never do," she heard him mutter in that irritating Hungarian accent of his.

How dare he?

She turned toward the wall. What he said was of course partly true. It could look like that, from the outside. Her life. But she didn't want him to say it. Didn't want him to feel that way. She was engaged in lots of things. The theater, literature... But at the same time, sitting with her head in her hands in the bathroom at the theater, despising everyone there, despising the production she was working on… how engaged was that? But how do you go about it? How? She shoved Loser down from the bed where he was kneading her with his paws in a futile attempt to get more food.

Tomorrow she would give up the notion of getting her own apartment and instead call the manager at a better theater. Tomorrow she would start her new life. Go up to Lincoln Center and borrow some books about theater history. Take her mother with her, she would like that. She was wide awake, angry and excited. Wanted to sleep. Tried to breathe calmly. Next to her Gabor was already asleep—on his back—snoring. She nudged him and turned toward the wall again.

9

Charles had already crawled into bed when Alice came out of the bathroom. Beside him he had put a black iron spear.

"Look, just like a knight."

She looked blankly at the spear.

"My Filipino spear I mean," he continued. "This will serve as a chastity wall between us. You needn't fear anything from me."

She sat suspiciously on the edge of the bed and picked up the spear.

"A Filipino spear. It looks real."

"It is real. It's a real head-hunting spear."

"A what?" Alice said, and withdrew her hand.

"It's a used head-hunting spear. From the northern Philippines. Bought it there a couple of years ago. Was at a darned nice wedding in Baguio."

"Well," she said quietly. "Secondhand, you say..."

She was silent for a moment.

"You know. We don't need this spear. I trust you. I guess I'm old enough to defend my own virtue."

He moved the spear to the floor.

"Swedish naivety."

Alice smiled and lay down beside him.

"And what would you know about that?"

He smiled back. "Good night, my dear," he said and turned off the light.

Outside the city was awakening.

Trucks started turning down streets to unload their goods at restaurants and retailers. Rats crept back into their holes, and beneath it all you could hear the subway through grates in the street from which steam billowed up and created its very own mystique. The soft cooing of pigeons was mixed with sirens.

And people who started work early were getting up.

And the water from their showers roared through the plumbing.

Alice lay awake with her back to Charles, listening to all the sounds of the city outside the apartment. Felt him, the stranger from an obscure, secret basement nightclub, move behind her.

"Alice. Are you awake?"

"Mmm," murmured Alice.

"I have something I want…"

He paused for a brief second then continued in a somewhat steadier voice.

"There is something I want to confess."

She stiffened but didn't turn around. Heard him breathing behind her. Then his voice came back from obscurity.

"My real name isn't Charles."

He said nothing more. Lay perfectly still behind her. She found herself wondering what horrible truth would be revealed by his real name. Pigeons cooed outside the window. She waited. Nothing was said. She felt no fear, but became impatient, wanted to know. Turned, looked at him as he lay there looking up at the ceiling.

"So what *is* your real name then?"

He took a deep breath and suddenly he wasn't speaking English, but rather Swedish with a Danish accent.

"My name is Carl, I come from Århus, to be exact."

He smiled to himself, turned his head and met her gaze. She giggled suddenly and stretched out her hand.

"Is that all?"

He nodded seriously.

For several minutes, she thought silently through the whole re-markable evening and then said slowly, as if to herself, "Tonight I met a Swede of Chinese origin. I met a young man from Hungary, one from Yugoslavia, a woman from Holland and now you from Denmark. Are there no Americans in America?"

"Not right here," said Carl.

And they lay there in the darkness looking at each other and smiled.

10

And a new day dawned.

It was time for all those city dwellers whose night is "day" to start the journey home. People who worked the night shift shared subway seats with those who were on their way to their day jobs. Hollow-eyed individuals crawled out of after-hours clubs where they'd been sitting at the bar back-to-back with a bunch of unscrupulous Wall Street types: well-groomed twenty-somethings who'd sneaked in for a small shot of night decadence on the way to their monotonous money management jobs. Maybe they joined others who were on their way from some secret club to a cocaine-infected late night party that continued well into the morning, until no illegal substance in the world could make anyone happy anymore and a long night could end up with a beautiful Miyake dress on a crushed body beneath the open window of a luxury loft.

But that doesn't belong in this story where an Alice from Äppelviken is fast asleep in the Italian tourist district—next to a Danish man who owns a used head-hunting spear.

Sometime shortly after eight o'clock on this morning, Babylonia and Gabor walked to the subway on Canal Street.

As usual, it took them time to make their way among all the vegetable stalls and novelty shops that already lined the street so early in the morning; simple wooden stands stacked with knockoffs of designer clothing, watches and handbags, next to kale, cilantro and gaping fish heads with empty eyes and the acrid smell of salt, sea and putrefaction.

Babylonia felt that last night's anxiety over starting with something new wasn't as urgent now in the smoggy yellow morning haze that hovered over Canal Street.

"It's like everything's at a standstill. I feel totally paralyzed," Babylonia tried to explain to Gabor. "Do you get the enormity of having your visiting mother go home with a complete stranger?"

Gabor smiled. "If you had met *my* mother you would really understand how incredible it *could* be... a retired lady with permed hair from a dilapidated palatial house in a Budapest suburb. Oh no, she would be completely out of place in the arms of a stranger in New York. But your mother? She's stylish, sleek, modernistic..."

"Modernistic? What the hell kind of expression is that?" Babylonia interrupted sharply. "Don't you understand? The thought of my mother in a beige suit asleep next to a stranger in some slummy apartment in New York... it just doesn't make any sense."

"Maybe you just don't know her..."

"Men's underwear on the floor, cockroaches, smelly refrigerator. No, I just can't..."

"Like I said, maybe you just don't know her."

"She's my mother. Of course I know her. I should know her. But this..." She cast an irritated glance at him as he lit a cigarette and with a small easy smile threw away the match. "This isn't funny, or even interesting, no matter how amusing you find it. It's simply quite disgusting."

"I think you're being unreasonable…" He grabbed her before she could step out into the street in front of a man who was hurriedly pushing a cart full of boxes, "And very narrow-minded. I think it's kind of nice."

"Nice? You're perverse. It's too much." She fell silent and thought that the entire idea of calling another theater manager, of making a change in her life…

It was simply overwhelming.

She couldn't bring herself to do it today.

It would have to wait until her mother returned to Sweden.

When they stopped at the red light near the entrance to the subway, Gabor put out his cigarette and muttered, "And… what about the apartment in Queens, then?"

"What?" she snapped, though she'd heard perfectly well what he'd just said. Not now! She looked down at the ground, at a puddle of smelly water in which cigarette butts were floating. Forgot what he said because she couldn't stop thinking about how insane it was that Alice went home with a complete stranger.

"The apartment in Queens. The one you were going to move to…"

"Obviously, I'm not going to do anything about that today."

And the feeling of her mother's presence in the city suddenly made her dizzy. Everything had come to a standstill. And to top it all off, her father might be on his way here too. He had been drunk when he called. She hoped he'd fallen asleep and that when he woke up he'd simply changed his mind.

II

Alice was awakened by the sound of pounding nearby. Opened her eyes, immediately knew where she was and sat straight up.

Next to her, Charles-Carl was peacefully asleep on his back with his arm slung over his eyes. He was snoring quietly with his mouth slightly open—a thin, unshaven, middle-aged man, a bit rickety perhaps, but with sensual lips. His upper lip was thin with a small scar, a straight upper lip without a clear Cupid's bow. He had beautiful lips. She bent over him gently, wanted to see him properly.

Imagine! She'd slept in his bed, breathed in his air...

She gasped.

The man had a tattoo on his shoulder!

So unexpected.

A lion's head with a paw under the chin.

She had never been involved with a man who was tattooed. Or had she, long ago? The Alice who slept with a young man in a tent on the beach in Tofta, the Alice who studied classical languages and civilizations, the single mom who baptized her daughter Babylonia. Could that Alice have been involved with someone who had a tattoo?

No, not even her.

Tattoos belonged to another class of people. But there he was now, asleep next to her, with a lion's head tattooed on his narrow shoulder.

She stood up and smoothed her blouse.

Everything was very odd indeed.

And her clothes were so wrinkled. It was the first time in her life that she'd slept fully dressed. He had offered her a T-shirt but she had declined. The sheets had smelled stale and she didn't want to get as close to him as what wearing his T-shirt would have meant.

She looked around the room. There was nothing there to suggest that women regularly came for a visit. But there was a strange smell, slightly musty, like a haystack.

Outside, birds were chirping. If she closed her eyes, she could pretend that she was at home in her own garden on an early spring morning. She wondered what kind of exotic birds could be living in the gray concrete courtyard outside the window, chirping so joyfully. There were no trees out there, after all.

She stood at the window, perfectly still, with her forehead against the glass but there were no birds in sight.

The chirping came from above.

She took a step back and looked up. High on a shelf against the window was a huge birdcage filled with tiny birds. Not your typical yellow or blue budgies. She would have recognized those. These were some other species. Small finches, perhaps.

She thought it was both strange and a bit repulsive. Watched the little green iridescent creatures in the cage high up by the window. Weird, that she hadn't heard or noticed them when she and Charles-Carl came in last night.

Silently, she sneaked into the bathroom. Lined the toilet seat carefully with toilet paper before she sat down. Looked around the small bathroom with its aqua green tiled walls. The black and white mosaic floor felt cold against the soles of her feet. While she peed, she had to admit that despite the peculiar birds and his surprising tattoo, it was exciting to be in a strange man's apartment. An *unfamiliar* can of shaving cream was on the ledge of the bathtub. With an *unfamiliar* razor beside it.

Life in Sweden felt like a distant dream—although it was this, the place she was in now, that should feel like a dream. Her life in the beautiful house in safe Äppelviken, that was "reality" and where she was now—a nightmare. But this apartment with its cage full of finches, the Danish man Carl with his bushy sideburns, lion tattoo and a used head-hunting spear—all this was undeniably a substantial part of the present reality.

She opened the medicine chest. A variety of headache pills, Band-Aids and a pair of nail scissors. But no tampons or condoms or anything else of a more private nature. Carefully, she washed her face and let her fingers glide over her hair. Wondered what it would be like to make love with him—in revenge, out of curiosity. Out of desire? Felt the same tingling sensation as when she first held Amanda's hand in her own. Like being curious, insecure, scared and excited all at the same time. Not like an adult in the midst of an acute life crisis with the capacity to review and analyze what was happening to her—no, rather like another kind of person altogether, an uncertain someone, with a brand new door *faintly* ajar.

The question was—did she really want to peek behind that door?

He was still asleep when she came out of the bathroom. The birds were now completely silent, as if they knew that she thought they were somewhat revolting.

The apartment's single room was filled from floor to ceiling with books. A simple television stood on a table at the foot of the bed, a bent metal coat hanger served as an antenna. There was an Art Deco table. It was the only beautiful piece of furniture in the otherwise rather shabby apartment. Though perhaps not really shabby after all. Aside from the strange birds, everything was neat and clean. The books were shelved in alphabetical order. Lots of literature in both French and German.

A rack of ties hung next to a small desk by the window. A small square Mac Plus was on the desk, with an IBM Selectric on the neighboring shelf. Could he be a journalist or a writer? That would explain why he'd been at that club last night. He seemed to be neither a nightclub connoisseur nor a gangster.

She went out into the small hall and put on her shoes and jacket.

I'm going to leave now, she thought. I may never know who he is, which is strange but also exciting.

She grabbed the doorknob and opened the door as quietly as she could, didn't hear the rustling of sheets behind her, the quiet feet crossing the wooden floor.

"I was going to let you slip away at first... but then I realized that I have no way to reach you."

She turned and there he stood in the doorway, draped in a blanket. "The only thing I know is that your name is Alice and you're from Stockholm. Do you dare give me your phone number?"

She touched her hair, confused. Number? She didn't know Babylonia's number by heart but she did have it on a slip of paper in her pocket. He wrote it down on the back of a Chinese takeout menu.

"When can I call?" Slowly, he took a step forward and kissed her lightly on the cheek. Nothing more. She closed her eyes and held her breath. They stood still. She felt the faint smell of the bird cage, mixed with the scent of him, a little dusty, a little sweaty.

She opened her eyes.

"It was very nice to meet you," he said gently.

She nodded.

"I would like to take you out to dinner before you go back to Sweden. If I may."

She nodded again.

He caressed her lightly on the cheek where his lips had just touched her.

"When I woke up, I was smiling," he said almost to himself. And with that, he cupped her face gently in his hands and kissed her lightly on the mouth.

At first she was scared. Then she relaxed into it, into this very moment, a moment that seemed like a strange dream, although it was actually reality, a reality in which she was kissing a strange man with bushy sideburns and a lion tattooed on his shoulder.

Completely without thinking—without allowing herself to think—she took his hand and they went back to bed. Lay down awkwardly next to each other. She still had on her shoes and jacket. It would get wrinkled, she thought fleetingly.

He unbuttoned her blouse, gently, one button at a time. She let him slip his hand under her back, let him undo her bra. She heard him gasp at the sight of her breasts. And as his lips searched out her nipples, for the first time in a very, very long time, she felt beautiful.

12

After Gabor got off at 8th Street, Babylonia stayed on the subway on the way to the office, thinking, "Who is this woman Alice really?" She had no idea.

Opposite her in the throngs of people heading to their jobs, a small baby was asleep in an umbrella stroller. A young black mother was holding the stroller tightly. The baby looked far too small for an umbrella stroller, thin fabric with no appreciable support for an infant's neck.

The young woman was listening to music on her Sony Walkman. Her head was bobbing in time to the music. Beside her sat a fat man, dressed in the traditional garb of Chassidic Jews, complete with long curly side locks. He was reading his holy book, lips moving in silence. The young mother and the Jewish man, from two different worlds, sat there next to each other. He with a firm grip on his book. The mother with a firm grip on the stroller, while she looked at nothing, absentmindedly.

She was young for being a mom. Merely a girl, much younger than I am, thought Babylonia. Like Alice back then? But who had the young Alice been? Who'd gotten pregnant in a tent in Gotland by someone, a stranger, a young man she said she never saw again. Naturally, Alice, the girl in the tent with the strange boy, must have been turned on, even thought it was hard for her, Babylonia, to sit here in this rattling subway car, and imagine her prudish mother being young and horny. And Alice hadn't really thought about the consequences of succumbing to her own desire. She hadn't thought about it, until she discovered that a new life was sprouting inside her.

Now here was Babylonia—the consequence of casual sex in a tent outside of Visby—riding the New York City subway, worrying about an Alice who, after a life on the periphery of her daughter's, had suddenly plunked herself down in the life Babylonia had created for herself. A completely foreign Alice, who just left all her stuff on the floor beside the vinyl couch... and then chose to spend the night with a complete and total stranger with no last name. A Charles, who—if Babylonia understood correctly—Alice had met at a roulette club. A roulette club! It was ridiculous. No way. Not in real life. Not in her mother's reality. She never set foot in gambling clubs.

Never ever.

As the subway rattled into the station, the young mother turned to Babylonia and met her gaze. Hostile and cold. As if the girl tightened her grip on the stroller when she felt Babylonia staring.

The Jewish man stood up and closed the book. And now she saw that it wasn't at all a holy book but rather a thriller, a Stephen King novel, as thick as a book of scripture. And out of the corner of her eye she saw the young mother caress the baby's cheek.

When the doors closed and the subway pulled out of the station, she met the girl's gaze again. This time, the girl smiled. Looked down at her child. Proud. The little smile curled her lips into a plump crescent. The baby slept peacefully in the uncomfortable stroller.

At the 51st Street station, Babylonia nodded towards the girl with the baby who nodded amicably back at her. Slowly, she made her way in the crowd up the stairs to the street. Found herself wishing that her father would show up after all and take care of everything. Take Alice home with him and stay there in the reality in which they belonged.

Dad, she thought, and smiled to herself. She loved him. Life without Göran was unimaginable, even though he wasn't her real father. But this fine non-biological father had baked bread that tasted like bread made on the continent. He had baked soft, German gingerbread cookies with a thin, white glaze.

Alice couldn't, or perhaps never wanted to, bake anything. Alice was always at the university or in her study. She worked! And sometimes her name appeared in the newspaper. Small articles about a scholarship or prize she'd won. There was never anything about Göran anywhere. He was just an ordinary businessman who sometimes did business in Berlin. But mostly, he had been at home, picked her up after school, been there.

And Babylonia had grown up in a world where mothers were absorbed by their work and dads could bake.

* * *

Göran stared at the clouds outside the window. Pressed the button and ordered another whiskey from the cute flight attendant. Maybe he'd walk to the back of the plane later and try chatting with her. He wanted to talk. Needed to talk. But how could he explain to anyone how things really were? How complicated it all was. There was no solution. And the very fact that he was sitting here on this plane was idiotic and no doubt a total mistake.

But like it or not, here he sat.

Would have to endure the consequences—or evade them.

If he could.

The whiskey arrived. He downed it.

* * *

At almost the same time—it's hard to pinpoint time in an aircraft that's traveling between time zones—Babylonia took a big sip of weak, vending machine coffee and picked up her binders at the Swedish import and export company. The office was ugly and desolate with overhead fluorescent lighting. A couple of dreary desks scattered on brown industrial carpeting. A poster of the King and Silvia on the wall.

It always smelled damp and dusty, of moldy paperwork.

She left a note on the manager's desk saying she'd be working from home today. Picked up the photo of his family that was displayed on his desk in a delicate blue and yellow striped porcelain frame. They smiled at the camera from a sailboat on an island in the Swedish archipelago. She studied his wife, tried to look into her eyes to see if this woman would ever follow two complete strangers into an illegal gambling club in a foreign city. But it was impossible to imagine such a thing behind those light blue, beady eyes that gazed calmly into the camera.

With the binders in her arms, she snuck out the door and into the elevator. Soon the clock would strike nine and the building would quickly fill up with office workers. She ducked behind a pillar when she saw her boss hurry past, left the building and walked towards the subway again.

Meanwhile, Gabor was sitting in a lecture hall, listless and tired and struggling to stay awake. The Korean movie they'd watched in class was filled with people who shot at each other, blood spurting everywhere. Gabor's only desire was for life to be beautiful. Preferably difficult and complicated—but beautiful. Without violence. Was that too much to ask for? He didn't think so.

And Alice? She still lay, in the closest possible intimacy, in a bed on Mulberry Street.

But Göran, for his part, had fallen asleep in his seat after another whiskey, blissfully unaware that a tattooed Danish man with bushy sideburns had just then finished gently making love to his wife—next to a slightly used head-hunting spear.

In the airline seat next to him, a woman in her sixties was also fast asleep. She was on her way to visit her newly married son in New Jersey, a young man who five months later would drive his Ford Taurus straight into the parapet above the waterfalls in the city of Patterson. But since this doesn't have anything with our story, we'll leave them there somewhere above Nova Scotia.

And what about Amanda—and Pavel? What were they doing?
    Well, what they were up to—right then?
    We don't want to know.

13

They sat down at a table in a small Italian outdoor cafe near Charles's building.

"You have to take the opportunity to sit outside when it's nice weather," he said and took her hand, opened her fingers and kissed her palm. Softly, with slightly moist lips. Alice withdrew her hand. Craned her neck, breathed in the air. Met her reflection in the store window next door. Disheveled, plain. But this feeling of being so unkempt, sticky, plain, disheveled. It didn't matter. She had never before felt that her appearance was as unimportant as it was right here and now. Here she sat, at an Italian sidewalk cafe on a street with the beautiful name Mulberry and it felt absolutely perfect to be this unkempt and sticky.

"You're really pretty," he said, and she surprised herself by actually believing him. She, Alice, 48. With very dirty disheveled hair, sticky all over but especially down there in the place she never really thought about in words. Vagina maybe, but did that word really signify? How do you name the thing that just existed down there, an opening that sometimes itched, but that right now was moist, sticky and a bit raw. Used.

She watched, fascinated, as Charles-Carl's practiced hands rolled a cigarette absentmindedly. Felt an urge to touch him. To reach out and grab his hand and kiss it as he had kissed hers. But she felt oddly shy now, even though she'd been so intimate with him. Just a short while ago.

At the table next to them a girl was reading. She was dark with thick shapely eyebrows. Her long slender legs were stretched in front of her, wound around a soft suede bag in nut brown.

Maybe it was the same girl who'd been there when Babylonia had breakfast at the cafe twenty-four hours earlier, or maybe it was another, similar girl. Who knows? Young people in New York can look dauntingly alike, no matter where they came from...

"They have no raspberry muffins here but good cappuccino and good cannoli, if you feel like something sweet," he continued, seemingly untouched by the incredible fact that they had made love though they didn't really know each other. Like two teenagers, just moments ago, up in his cramped warm apartment that smelled of caged birds, on sheets that should have been laundered weeks ago.

He sat with his head bent over his cigarette and she wanted to say something so it wouldn't feel like a thick strained wall of silence between them now, after that incredible thing had taken place, after his tongue had sought out the most intimate parts of her body. Just the fact that she'd dared show him her body in the merciless daylight up there in his bed. That *was* incredible.

Used.

Shamelessly pleasured.

"Do you ever get home to Denmark?" she said simply.

He lit his cigarette.

"I used to. When my parents were still alive," he replied, and took a deep drag. She coughed lightly and he moved the cigarette to his other hand, a little further away from her. But he didn't put it out.

Two small cups of cappuccino, with brown cinnamon sprinkled on top, were set down in front of them. Charles searched his pockets for money and eventually produced a crumpled bill from his pants pocket.

The coffee was good and the taste made Alice feel closer to her usual self. She skimmed her spoon over the light brown foam that floated on the surface and looked around. This was a nice street, lined with trees and Italian cafes. You could hear children's voices from a school playground down the street. She thought it felt like a real street, a street where ordinary people lived. It felt good.

"Don't you have any family left in Denmark?" She hoped it wouldn't sound as if she were trying to interrogate him. But he just smiled a little, leaned forward and touched her hand with his index finger.

"Family. Nope. Only a brother and a crabby sister-in-law. They have a house in the suburbs, two cars and two teenage children. I've invited them to visit but they'd rather vacation at some boring resort. They think that I live an undignified life, you see."

"Undignified?"

Alice could see her own house in Äppelviken in front of her. The two cars. Her neighbors in a similar house.

"I have no pension and no income from sources they understand. I've had other priorities. When I go home, they just try to convince me that I want what they want." He smiled and blew out a perfectly shaped smoke ring.

"And I've never wanted that..." He leaned toward her again, looked deeply into her eyes. "But the older I get, well, I don't know. The idea of growing old here scares me sometimes."

"Why would it scare you? It's nice here." She looked around. Across the street was an old-fashioned barbershop. Further down, a pretzel hung outside a shop. A bakery? Yes, this was a friendly street. Like a street from another era. "It would be nice to live here as an old person," she said hesitantly.

He drank some of his coffee. "Sure. But I might wind up alone when I'm old. And without a proper lease, I have no rights as a tenant. Everything is changing and soon I won't be able to afford to live here. I could wind up living in a cardboard box on the street, who knows."

"A cardboard box on the street? No way. You're an adult."

He smiled. "Adult. It sounds boring. Adult?" He was trying the word on for size. "Maybe. But I'm living in a society where I don't exist. I have no papers." He scratched himself absently on the calf.

She looked down, no papers? Was he saying that he lived here illegally? What did that mean? He was Danish. You didn't walk around with no papers if you had any order in your life. No, he was too mysterious. She looked away. Suddenly wanted to be someplace else. Everything about him was too vague. Paperless!

But then it suddenly struck her, a raw and honest insight: She *wanted* to see him again. Hadn't even dared to fully enjoy their love making. Hadn't let herself go. Just teetered on the brink of the deep abyss that orgasms had been in her marriage to... what was his name again? Göran. Yes. That was it. In another life. But if she dared to see this illegal immigrant from the country of Denmark again—if she did—would it be for her own sake or for the sake of revenge?

"What are you thinking?" he asked and she blushed.

"About being alone," she lied. "What did you mean by that?"

"Oh," he said. "It wasn't that interesting. Maybe it's just about where you belong. Later. When you're old."

She wanted to say something wise but didn't have time to think up a sufficiently well-formulated thought before he continued.

"I'm scared that I'll turn into a sad, foreign man sitting in a cardboard box on the street, mourning my lost nationality. Smørrebrød and Carlsberg. Well, you know how things can go."

"No," she said. "I don't."

She watched him as he sat across from her, pensive, with the coffee cup in his hand. She would not be able to relocate him into the garden in Äppelviken, but he fit in here. And then, just then—NOW—she felt that in this very moment with him, every little part of her body felt *alive*. This street. This cafe. This cappuccino. The intimate lovemaking with him—*how* would she ever be able to drag herself back to her regular life, in that house back home, a life that now seemed so indescribably burdensome?

She leaned forward.

"But there's nothing wrong with being an old foreign man here. What would be so sad about that?"

"That your whole life has been one big mistake, that you've been living the wrong life, in the wrong place. That you suddenly realize that you belong neither in the new country nor in the old one. You know…"

"No." She hesitated. "Perhaps I've never felt that I fit in."

He raised his strangely shaped eyebrows.

"Have you lived abroad for any length of time then?"

"No. Just in the western suburbs of Stockholm my entire life."

"I chose to move out into the world." He leaned back. "But now, well, you change your mind. Everything I despise and think is boring about Denmark is starting to feel more like my true self—my Danish roots are starting to grow in my aging New York body."

He smiled, embarrassed, and put out a half-smoked cigarette, seemed suddenly insecure. "No, now I'm just being pretentious. Forget what I said. I am happy here."

He had a small stain on his jacket sleeve. She wanted to bend forward and rub it away. Felt… tenderness. But just sat quietly with her coffee and smiled, moved aside to make room for a dark-skinned young mother pushing a child in an impractical stroller with wheels too small to get around comfortably on the rough and worn pavement.

"Anyway—it's painful, you know. Not belonging in your own reality no matter where you are." He lit another cigarette. "So the conclusion is that you should stay at home. Marry a neighborhood girl, your childhood sweetheart. Or someone you met randomly in a tent at a festival some summer. Then life would be simple."

His smile broadened and he leaned toward her. Was Charles from the bed again, where *it* had happened. Suddenly uncomfortable, she averted her eyes and looked around.

Somewhere nearby, by a window a few floors up, a man was singing. His rich operatic voice drifted up and down a scale, changed keys, up again and down... now a key higher but still the same thing... eight tones up and then eight tones down again. The scales created a pattern, an order...

The voice was beautiful.

She closed her eyes.

Charles put his hand over hers.

"I have to go to work for a couple of hours. Can I call you later?"

Work? Of course. Reality. Even a man like Charles must of course have a job.

All around them the city roared. The city where everyone always worked, whether it was practicing scales with a voice oiled by tea and honey; or putting in fourteen hour days of pointless administration in offices filled with randomly scattered desks, cluttered with paperwork and sticky triplicate forms that needed to be filed; or endless days at ramshackle sewing machines, with or without union membership. Wherein lies the difference really—except for in salary? The workdays were still longer than anything Alice could have imagined. After all, this was the city where there were lots of odd jobs so that everyone had an opportunity. The city where three men operated the boom to a simple bridge over a shimmering green channel in Brooklyn. The city where people worked in hundreds of tiny dusty toll booths. The city where stores were always open, where police cars and fire trucks were always on the move, their sirens blaring around the clock, drowning out the church bells. The city where people consequently sought peace and quiet by buying countless numbers of books about alternative lifestyles. Spiritual books, which they then stacked in stressful piles on their bedside tables.

But Alice hadn't discovered any of this yet, as she sat at the cafe on the street with the beautiful name, Mulberry, with the Danish man, Charles. He who claimed he had no papers.

"What do you do?" she asked.

He thought for a moment and replied slowly:

"I sort facts."

"You do what?"

"Facts-on-File. I sort facts, newspaper clippings. Everything is then archived. If there's something you need to know, you call us. We have all the published facts. Everything you want to know, archived from A to Z, or A to Ø, as we say back home."

She liked the idea of sorting facts. It pleased her.

"But can you make a living doing that?"

"More or less. It pays the rent and my fairly simple habits. I used to have expensive habits. Was a compulsive gambler for fifteen years. But I'm totally clean now."

"Really," she said, and they sat in silence for a while.

Charles stood up and gave Alice a quick hug.

"I have to go. Will you find your way? Take a taxi otherwise."

She looked around.

"I'll be fine. I have the little map you lent me."

"Take a taxi."

"I promise... if I get lost."

"Don't."

He kissed her on the cheek. His scent was already familiar. They stood, foreheads touching, for a moment. Then he stretched, caressed her lightly on the cheek, waved goodbye and got ready to start walking north.

She walked a few steps in the opposite direction. Then she turned and shouted after him.

"Charles. Carl."

He turned in the middle of a small strutting step and raised his eyebrows. It felt as if she had disturbed him. His thoughts were already elsewhere.

"Yes."

"What's your last name?"

He took a couple of strides back and stretched out his hand, took hers and shook it with a firm grip.

"Claessen."

She pondered this and told him her last name, while they gravely shook hands with each other. Now formally introduced.

"Wait a minute. What's your brother's name?" She held her breath.

"Morten. Why?"

"It was nothing," she said quietly but felt infinitely disappointed. Imagine if it had been him. The Danish boy from that summer when Babylonia was conceived. But no.

She waved and walked away, not seeing how he stood there watching her.

14

A tired and worn out Amanda, wearing giant sunglasses, opened the gates outside the door to the bar called BAR. Two old men stood by the door and waited. Today was Friday and the bar would be open for lunch. Otherwise, even regulars like they are would have to wait until evening. They walked slowly into the darkness behind Amanda, sat down and waited for her to be ready to serve them their liquid lunch.

Henry, who had helped Alice down from the fire escape, stood and smoked outside the entrance to his shop. The heat and stench of garbage was nearly as putrid as during the worst heat of summer. He wiped his forehead and nodded towards Babylonia who was walking by with her arms full of binders. She nodded back. Wondered as usual why this particular Chinese man acknowledged her, greeted her. To all the others, she was just a ghost they looked straight through. She could feel it when she went into the little shop down the street to buy milk or toilet paper. If any Chinese customers were there at the same time, it was as if she became invisible. Sometimes, people on the street bumped right into her. As if she were a ghost. A white ghost in Chinatown.

* * *

Alice hadn't gone more than a block when she felt someone walking beside her. Someone who walked at the same pace, calmly, almost as if they were intentionally walking together.

She looked up to meet a brilliant smile from Pavel's wide mouth with its sparse, yellow teeth. She could glimpse his intense, somewhat deranged eyes behind his fake black Ray-Bans. Like her, he looked like he'd slept in his clothes.

"Good morning, darling," he said and put his big hand on her arm. His grip forced her to stand still. Alice looked around, but no one seemed to notice that she'd been stopped by a burly man in wrinkled clothes.

"How nice to run into you like this," he said and leaned down. He was so gigantic that he almost had to bend in half to give her a kiss on the cheek. Without meaning to, she held up her hand to keep him at bay. He smelled strongly of cigarettes, bad teeth and a pretty good aftershave, which didn't really fit in with the rest of his appearance and momentarily confused her. As if the scent of the cologne indicated a different man than the one she was looking at.

"And where did you disappear to last night, with all the money?"

"The money?" She had forgotten about the money.

"If I remember correctly, my dear, the last time I saw you, you had a pretty hefty wad of cash that belonged to me."

She gasped. "What on earth are you talking about?" She looked around and lowered her voice to a whisper. "*You* left me with a bunch of *gangsters*." She had to stand on tiptoe to be sure that he would hear. "I have no money. No one was allowed to leave with the money, you see."

"Gangsters?" He smiled broadly and scratched his ear. "You don't say? Yet I just saw you with a guy who *I* know has good connections."

"Connections?"

"Contacts. Useful acquaintances. Of all kinds. You know what I mean..."

"No, I don't know."

She had to step out into the street to make way for a man with a cart full of groceries that he'd unloaded from a small pickup truck. Pavel didn't move. Grumbling, the man pushed the cart around him and Alice had to move again. Irritated, she turned her face up toward his angular face and said loudly, not bothering to whisper, "I don't know what you're talking about, Pavel. I'm so tired. We'll talk later, in peace and quiet when Amanda is around. Everything was very strange last night."

She began to walk down the street but, once again, he grabbed her arm and held her so that she couldn't move, helpless as a limp rag doll in his grasp.

"Did he get my money? The guy with the contacts. Was he there last night?"

"I said I wasn't allowed to keep any money. Didn't you hear what I said?"

"I heard well enough. But you just disappeared," he replied languidly.

Just then, a messenger came biking by without a thought of yielding to them. Alice stumbled to the side, felt something on the bike scratch her leg, looked down, saw the scratch, blood. Not much, not much blood at all, but the combination of the little red streak of her own blood and the sting that accompanied it, made her dizzy and nauseous. Pavel was unmoved by any of this, steady as a lamppost in the middle of the sidewalk gripping her arm firmly. She tore herself away.

"You'll have to excuse me, but I can't talk to you about this anymore. I'm tired and just want to put yesterday behind me and check into a nice hotel. Goodbye."

She started to walk a little faster towards bustling Canal Street, where Little Italy almost imperceptibly began to merge with Chinatown. Previously, Canal Street served as a sharp boundary between Manhattan's Chinatown and Little Italy. But not anymore. Now Italian restaurants could be seen next door to Chinese vegetable stands.

Alice waited impatiently at the pedestrian crossing at the corner of Mulberry and Canal. Traffic stood still for no visible reason other than too many cars headed in the same direction at the same time. The sidewalks on Canal Street were packed with stalls where you could buy everything from imitation Gucci bags to the most exotic fish and spices. Everyone was in a hurry, drivers in the stationary cars honked irritably at each other. The air was still and heavy, trapping the exhaust fumes, forcing her to inhale them. She held her hand up to her mouth and tried to filter out the oxygen.

"Well, you don't have to get so angry. Or walk so fast. I'm running out of breath. We're headed in the same direction." The familiar voice was now velvety, close to her ear.

Without looking up at Pavel, in an attempt to make it clear that she wanted to be left alone, she picked up the little map that Charles had lent her. It was easy. Left on Canal Street and then diagonally across the Bowery, until she reached Catherine Street. She would find her way.

But Pavel had other ideas. He grabbed her hand and pulled her across Canal Street through the stationary traffic and exhaust fumes, into tourist-Chinatown. "Let's take a shortcut." They entered Mott Street, a narrow street lined with touristy Chinese restaurants. They all looked alike, decorated with red lanterns and large billboards proclaiming their Peking duck the best in New York, or that they used no MSG in their cooking.

She let herself be led for a couple of blocks. Pavel's hand held hers in a tight grip, and felt rough and sticky. She wondered how long it had been since he'd last washed. He smelled. And not just of cologne—but of clothing that was never thoroughly washed, with detergent in a proper washing machine, with pre-wash and an hour long wash cycle. The smell was horrible and his hand was disgusting. She could imagine what his nails looked like, as they pressed into her palm. She started to gag and the taste of vomit filled her mouth.

At a corner, they had to step aside for a procession of tourists filing behind a guide with a flag in his hand. She seized the opportunity to tear her hand out of his grasp, turned and ran down a narrow alley. Into a courtyard. A door stood open. She snuck in, stood there in the darkness and waited.

Outside Pavel hurried past. He stopped when he came into the courtyard, looked around, and went back out to the street again.

She breathed a sigh of relief.

This was ridiculous. Why was she even afraid of him? She was just so incredibly tired. That was it. Had to pick up her bag and check into a hotel. Wanted to brush her teeth, rinse her mouth with mouthwash, that wonderful taste of *clean.* And then—sink into a neat, soft bed with down pillows in an air conditioned room.

She stretched and scratched her hand a little where his recent grip had felt sweaty and disgusting. Was about to go out into the daylight again, when she heard a noise behind her. Clothing rustling, the clang of something metallic falling to the floor. She turned around.

Two teenage Chinese boys sat in the dark examining something shiny. They met her gaze and looked bewildered.

She froze.

The boys looked at each other and then one of them cleared his throat and asked, "Are you a cop, ma'am?"

"Am I what?" she replied confused.

"You're not a cop, are you?"

"I'm Swedish," replied Alice.

The boys looked at each other and then down at what they had between them in the dark. She couldn't see what it was, but sensed that it was something shiny and pointed.

Reality suddenly became crystal clear. The stairwell with its filth and its flaws seemed illuminated. Everything was completely logical, like being in a dream where you suddenly find yourself on a tightrope high above a circus audience.

She gulped.

One of the boys stood up.

"Don't worry, lady," he said. "I'm not going to buy it. I'm just looking."

"What the...?" said the other teenager in surprise and pulled at his buddy's pants so that he would sit down again.

She felt the laughter bubbling up inside her, couldn't push it down. It slipped out of her.

"Are you okay?" continued the first teenager. "Are you lost?" His gaze drifted from his friend back to the nervous, laughing woman. "Or do you have some business in this building?" he continued calmly.

The other boy muttered something angrily in Chinese. The first shoved him and turned to Alice again. "Listen, lady, this isn't a hair salon or a shop for tourists. Maybe you're looking for the acupuncture clinic?"

She felt herself nodding. Acupuncture clinic. Sure. That made logical sense.

"In that case, I can show you where it is, just three doors down to the right." He put down the bundle with the long, shiny contraption on the window sill and stood up throwing a sharp glance at his friend.

Alice backed out into the courtyard.

"Don't be afraid. There's nothing to be afraid of. I'm just going to point you in the right direction."

He took her arm and led her out into the street again, where a group of Italian tourists walked by, busy talking and laughing, seeing nothing more than what they wanted to see.

"Look." The boy pointed down the street. "There, you see the sign? That's the acupuncture clinic. Have a nice day now, ma'am." He disappeared into the alley again.

Alice felt her heart pounding—as if it were running in her chest. Wanted to get away, though she stood rooted to the ground, perfectly still. Wanted to get far away from Chinese teenagers with their sharp, shiny secrets, away from gigantic Balkan men who demanded... well, what was it he wanted, really? It was so absurd. Pavel wanted money that she, Alice Berglund, 48 years old, from Äppelviken, Sweden had won in an illegal gambling club in a cellar under a bridge in lower Manhattan.

Things like that did not happen.

Not to her.

Not ever.

She began to walk down the street, staggered, turned a corner where she could be invisible. In safety. But her legs began to tremble. Her knees buckled, stability and control all gone.

Across the street was a small desolate playground, completely empty, except for one elderly man sleeping on a bench. A child's bucket and shovel lay abandoned beside the swings.

She sank down on an empty and worn bench with no backrest, at a safe distance from the bench with the sleeping old man. His possessions were tightly packed into a shopping cart next to him.

Was she going mad? Imagining danger in every situation? She wasn't even sure if she had seen something potentially dangerous, or if she was afraid of two ordinary teenagers in stairwell tinkering with a tool—just an ordinary tool. She was behaving like a paranoid lunatic. She had to calm down. She closed her eyes and concentrated on her breathing. Just sat there, shutting out the city and listened to herself instead. Her heartbeat, her lungs, the blood that flowed in her veins... and the panic that was rising...

Breathe, breathe, breathe. Just remember to breathe.

She was overwhelmed again by the desire to shower, brush her teeth, put on clean clothes and drive to work. To think about concrete things like work—not about something as broad and abstract as her entire meaningless life.

What was she doing here?

She wanted to go home. But what was home—now? And her work—what significance did it really have? Everything that had been obvious, that she had taken for granted when she was younger, her research, her ideas and structures. Everything now felt meaningless and trivial.

But what was left then?

Nothing.

She held her head in her hands. How could she, a mere fifteen minutes ago, there on Mulberry Street, have let herself be fooled into feeling alive just because she'd had an adventure?

It was no adventure—just a shabby affair.

Nevertheless, the thought of Charles, even of his little sordid apartment, made something inside her begin to blossom, and in the midst of all this anxiety and emptiness she suddenly found herself smiling.

* * *

A few minutes later, as Alice stood up and started walking over toward Catherine Street, the two Chinese boys were running down Mott Street. They carried something big and unwieldy between them in a brown paper bag. No one gave them a second thought. So we leave them there—for now...

On the sixth floor at 120 Catherine Street, Elvis and Loser were fighting on the kitchen mat, while Babylonia put down her binders on the kitchen table. Elvis got bored when Loser failed to put up a fight, so he majestically sat down in the open kitchen window and licked his paws. Maybe he was thinking about taking a little walk there on the windowsill.

And where had Pavel gone when Alice ran and hid? Well, he hadn't bothered to look for her, instead he sauntered through Chinatown, across the Bowery, down Catherine Street and sat down at the bar called BAR where Amanda poured him a Miller draft—even though he clearly and explicitly had asked for a large Pilsner Urquell. But you can't have everything you ask for. And the beer was free.

In other words, everything in the big city rolled on.

And at that very moment, an airport bus arrived at gate 45, on the top floor of the gigantic bus terminal.

A steady stream of passengers climbed out of the bus. Most people carried suitcases. Among the first to get off was Göran.

Out of nowhere, little Mister Man showed up. He took a firm hold of Göran's bag. Göran nodded gratefully and followed Mister Man down through the labyrinth of escalators.

15

Alice's hair! It was the first thing Babylonia noticed.

Her hair, usually so neatly styled, was now uncombed, disheveled, perhaps even matted. Like the hair of a homeless person.

And she wore no stockings.

Her jacket was wrinkled.

And when Babylonia just stood there in the doorway without letting her in, Alice started to laugh.

At first, Babylonia said nothing, hadn't ever heard her mother laugh that way. Her regular mother, the one who lived in Äppelviken, did not laugh uncontrollably. That mother lectured seriously. Was always dryly factual—lectured and taught. But now this very same mother was standing in a stairwell in Chinatown laughing hysterically.

"Mom, what happened?"

No answer.

She opened the door and let this transformed mother in.

Alice, who now stopped laughing, stepped in but said nothing, just stood and looked toward the window where Elvis balanced on the windowsill outside the kitchen window. The cat looked lazily into the depths below the window, made a complete circle on the narrow ledge six floors above ground. Took a couple of light, confident strides. Seemed to brazenly enjoy the feeling of intimidating the two women who were watching him, while he was completely calm himself. Secure in the feline knowledge that he hadn't risked anything at all with his balancing act. Everything was completely under control. Without condescending to even look at them, he sat gracefully down by the open window and licked himself pleasurably and carefully between the claws of his front paws.

"Mom, what's happened?" repeated Babylonia.

Alice turned to her and said slowly, "Well, the last thing that happened was that I watched an arms deal in a stairwell—I think."

She sat down.

"It's been a bit much."

"Arms deal? Mom, now you're hallucinating. Selling weapons is illegal here."

The smell of cockroaches, a licorice-like odor from the roach traps, felt stuffy in the heat of the kitchen. And the cat litter smelled sour. I ought to change it, Babylonia thought, tired. Outside the door, someone was going down the stairs, muttering in Chinese.

"I'm exhausted," said Alice. "Can you please make me a cup of tea?"

Babylonia opened the cupboard door and picked up the only tea she had, generic tea bags from one of the supermarket chains. Lousy tea! And she was fully aware that her mother, the regular mother who lived in Äppelviken, meant tea leaves of good quality, preferably brewed in a pot, preferably a pot decorated with English flowers. Suddenly, she realized how angry, how incredibly angry, she was at her mom and those fucking English floral cups.

"Dad might be sitting on a plane on his way here," she snapped and felt mean for wanting to shake her mother up. But she couldn't stop feeling irritated all over. And, truth to be told, she didn't know for sure. Absolutely not. She hadn't heard from him again, not since he had slurred in the middle of the night that he was on his way. But right now she wished that her mother would appreciate the mess she'd made of everything

Alice took off her suit jacket and smoothed it out.

"Why?"

Babylonia got a hanger, took the jacket from Alice and hung it up.

"I think you should tell me what exactly happened. He said you'd had a breakdown and let your imagination run away with you. That you needed a rest."

"He said that? Rest? He is nuts."

Alice stood up.

Babylonia wished she felt like hugging her, wanted to *want* to get them to talk more about it. About what had happened at home in Äppelviken. But was it even possible to talk about your parents' personal problems, to conduct a war council about your mother's demons? Did she even want to know that her mother was wavering, was maybe even losing it? Wouldn't she herself drown if she tried to keep her mother afloat?

"I'd like to take a shower," Alice said and took a deep breath. "Is that okay?" She pointed at the bathtub next to the kitchen table. "If your father shows up here, I don't want to see him. Not now. I'll check into a hotel."

"Mom," whispered Babylonia, "You look terrible. What happened, exactly?"

She turned off the kettle before it could start whistling. Alice stood up.

"I'll tell you later when I've showered and put on some clean clothes."

Suddenly, her voice was back to normal. "And what about that tea?"

"What were you thinking?" Babylonia said and stared down at the package of tea. "What did you imagine you'd accomplish by just showing up here? He said you just left. That you didn't say anything. You never do anything without planning."

"What would you know about that?"

Alice didn't want, had no energy left, to talk with her daughter about what happened back home. Not now. She didn't want to get angry now. Felt that somewhere deep down the adventure she had would fuel her through the day: Charles, the club, Amanda and Pavel. Roulette! *She'd played roulette at an underground club.* She giggled again and felt how Babylonia turned and stared at her as if she were drunk.

"Mom, are you all right? Gabor has Valium if you want."

"Valium. Beloved child, no thanks."

Would life never start to feel normal again? Although she had returned to her daughter's apartment, everything felt even more distorted—as if the world was slowly, well... tilting. Not much, but there was nothing to stand firmly on. And in the middle of this surreal world she stood—and was offered Valium. As if that would solidify the ground under her feet.

* * *

At the same time, on 49th Street near Seventh Avenue, Charles stepped into a long black limousine with dark windows. It had surprised him as it stood waiting for him with the engine softly humming outside the entrance to the Facts-On-File office.

He was driven through the heavy Midtown traffic back south along Broadway.

At the intersection of Broadway and 34th Street, completely unaware of one another, the taxi carrying Alice's husband Göran passed Charles's long black car.

But this coincidence is not important to our story. It's just one of those things that happen in a big city.

* * *

Babylonia set the tea and some cups on the table. Had purposely chosen two mismatched cups, served the milk out of the container. Wanted to demonstrate that her routines here were different than the ones at home in Äppelviken. She slammed the cups down on the table, wanting to be just slightly bohemian.

And she didn't want to drink tea.

She wanted to pour two large glasses of flowery mellow Brooklyn Lager, and take her mother up to the roof. Who needed glasses anyway? It was tastier to drink right out of the bottle. But Alice would no doubt think it was too early in the day for alcohol: "It's a weekday." So unimaginative, the way things were done in Äppelviken. Tea from floral teapots, wine with your meals only on the weekend, well-ironed underwear that no one ever saw, folded in perfect piles in drawers. All those meaningless rules.

Everything that she disliked about her childhood was now catching up with her. Was sitting across from her at the table, staring down in confusion at the mismatched cups without any saucers.

Alice quietly lifted the cup to her lips.

"Aren't you interested in hearing what Dad had to say?" asked Babylonia sharply.

"Not especially. Strangely enough."

"What happened? Are you just tired of each other? Are you going through some sort of midlife crisis?"

"Was *that* what he said?"

"Yes, more or less…"

"He should talk."

Babylonia sat down opposite her. "Why do you say that? Something *did* happen."

Alice sat still and looked at the tea in the cup that didn't match the other cup. Without a saucer. And it was as if Äppelviken and Sweden were behind a thick impenetrable spruce hedge. Pavel, Chinatown and Charles formed filters between her and her life back home. She couldn't open the door to her Swedish self. But she gave it a try.

"The fact that he isn't your biological father…"

Babylonia countered directly. "He IS my father. I've never had anyone else."

"No, of course not. Your real father. It's just biology. But…"

"He sounded very worried. Said you were…" She hesitated. "Have you had some kind of breakdown, Mom?"

"Did he say that?"

Babylonia nodded

"And he said nothing more?"

"No."

They sat in silence.

"He's been cheating on me… or rather, he's had a long relationship that I *just* found out about."

It felt empty when she said it.

"It's not true. I don't believe it," Babylonia said slowly.

"Yes, it is." Alice leaned forward and patted her cheek. "It sounds pathetic. I understand that. Stuff happens when you've been together for twenty years."

"But he can't just have had an affair without further notice. You've probably drifted apart. You're always working."

Alice sat quietly, stirring her tea.

"I don't think he's on his way here, honey. Although it sounds nice. He was going away again today… yesterday, I mean. To her I presume. In Berlin."

She looked down at her hands where the wedding ring still graced her left hand.

"What feels most remarkable is not knowing who I was married to. That we never traveled to Berlin together, for example, never shared his life there."

Babylonia stood up, eager to light a cigarette, but didn't want to smoke in front of her mother. "*You* haven't been in Berlin," she said prickly. "You were always so busy, but I've been there, several times."

If only they had been sitting with a beer instead of this bad tea, she thought. She didn't want to take sides. Had always been daddy's girl. And mother Alice was always so distant, aloof, living in a bubble that neither Babylonia nor her father had ever managed to penetrate.

"There were never any women," she continued. "There were only a bunch of boring meetings in hotel bars. Cigars. Old men in stiff suits."

All she could actually remember was that they had stayed in a nice hotel, the largest hotel she had ever seen. Or maybe it wasn't all that big. She couldn't quite remember... now.

But—this had been in West Berlin, and there had been another world in that city too; an East Berlin, that they had passed through while riding the subway. Empty ghost stations that the train just whizzed past so that no one from there would get the chance to board. All they saw was the occasional soldier with a machine gun, guarding an abandoned subway station. As if that eastern world didn't exist—if everyone simply turned a blind eye. As if her entire childhood could be picture perfect if she just closed her eyes. Even Dad's Berlin.

She sat down again. "I never saw him paying special attention to anyone there. Are you really sure, Mom?"

"I've seen a note and a photo. I've talked to his friend Dieter. Yes, I'm sure."

She drank the last of the tea, stood up. "I want to get dressed before your boyfriend comes home. Then maybe we can see about a hotel."

Babylonia saw Alice stop at the roach trap on the counter. She picked it up. Read the label: "*Roach Motel, roaches check in but they never check out.*" She quickly put it down again and glanced at Babylonia without saying a word.

Babylonia remained seated in the kitchen, staring at the Roach Motel, her newspaper, her cat and Gabor's irritating canvas shoes scattered on the floor. The whole world shrank around her. Her mother consumed all the air in the apartment.

If only she would have been at home yesterday, had answered the call from Alice and had managed to prevent everything from happening—or at least have had time to prepare herself.

Time to book a hotel.

Get a haircut.

Arrange her schedule.

Find herself another job.

Acquire a more impressive boyfriend.

Make more interesting friends

Reserve a table at that restaurant in Central Park—what was it called again?

Simply been able to present something other than her actual life.

She wished that her mother could see the magic in her city. Not only the Roach Motels, the cracked floorboards, the flaking paint on the damaged walls. She wished that they had been able to go up to the roof together last night. Drink beer or wine together and be dazzled by the big city with its powerful buildings and smells, the hum of so many people's lives. All the impressions that almost overwhelmed you with their zest for life.

She didn't know that her mother had stood up there yesterday and experienced all those things herself. That the magic, the city's magic, had struck her mother as much as it struck her and that Alice now, at this very moment, was in the other room trying to process the enormous mass of experiences, events, circumstances that were coasting through her otherwise so calm and proper existence. Was in a state of shock that wouldn't let go, simply got more and more bewildering.

Babylonia got up and followed her into the other room.

Alice stood there in the middle of the room and stared down into her open bag.

Completely naked.

There she stood, middle-aged and naked, in a room on Catherine Street, crying.

Silently.

Babylonia got scared. This was more frightening than when Alice had stood at the door and laughed. She wasn't supposed to be the kind of mother who laughs or cries. She was supposed to be a mother who's always there and makes your decisions for you. Simple decisions like what foreign language you should study in high school or what you should pack for lunch. Her mother—no one's mother—should ever stand naked in one's apartment in New York City with disheveled just-got-laid hair and cry.

Without saying a word, Babylonia locked herself in the bathroom and felt herself filling up with something like horror, or perhaps resignation, and the worst thing was that she couldn't cry.

* * *

And naturally it was precisely at this moment that the intercom rang, sharp and shrill.

Standing down there was the ethereal, if faintly worn, Amanda. Her shoulder-length dark hair blew aside, revealing a slender white neck with a small tattoo of a star. Her thin black coat fluttered around her body, and she radiated a quality granted a rare few in this world. A fascinating aura that, if she had used it, could have led her to places completely different from Catherine Street.

Henry Andersson-Chu stood across the street and watched her silently, admiringly. Just as puzzled as Babylonia as to why this beautiful creature worked in the dark, smelly bar down there on the corner.

Amanda pressed the button again, the only intercom button at 120 Catherine Street that did not have an Asian name. She wanted to be sure that Alice had gotten home safely. To make sure that the austere woman who'd had a little too much to drink last night, hadn't run into trouble.

She had, after all, slipped away into the dark night. Disappeared without anyone noticing.

So Amanda rang the intercom, pressed the button next to two handwritten names, names that looked European. But no one answered. Babylonia was sitting on the toilet six flights up, head cradled in her hands, and Alice was still standing naked in the middle of the room crying—silently.

When no one answered, Amanda walked slowly back to the bar called BAR where she'd left Pavel minding the store.

It was pretty quiet in there. Melvin and Bob, the two haggard re-tirees, were the only customers. They each had a little gin and tonic in front of them that they nursed as long as possible. They sat there at the bar called BAR, hanging out without really talking to each other, like they did every day until their social security money ran out.

16

At midday, the sunbeams reached all the way down to Catherine Street. They danced in the shimmering green, stinking puddles and bounced off the glass on the shop windows, the same windows that the shop owners struggled to keep clean from dust and exhaust fumes.

The only shop that still displayed a sign in Yiddish had already closed for Shabbat. Maybe it was a special Friday. It was after all fall, when many of the major Jewish holidays fell. But the Chinese vegetable sellers didn't care. They followed a different calendar and celebrated other holidays. They drowned each other out shouting in Cantonese or Mandarin as they unloaded their merchandise, wooed customers and swept their stalls.

Alice stood in the living room and looked out the window. She was sweaty and hot, uncomfortable in her turtleneck sweater. She hadn't imagined that September could be so humid and warm. Had packed all the wrong clothes in the rush, in that unreal reality on the other side of the Atlantic.

Then.

But now was now, and tomorrow she would go to a high-end department store and buy silk blouses.

Or just go home.

Back.

If he was on his way here.

Down on the street Henry stood on his own, smoking. She took the opportunity to wave to him when he glanced up at her building. He squinted, shading his eyes with his hand, and when he saw it was her, he waved cheerfully back.

Li Ming stepped out of the fabric store and waved to Alice too. Alice smiled and waved back.

Babylonia was watching her from the door.

"Who are you waving to?"

"My friends."

"What do you mean, friends?"

Babylonia stuck her head out the window. Gabor was walking down the street wheeling his bike. Alice waved to Gabor, but he didn't see her. Babylonia shook her head and walked to the kitchen.

Alice waved once more down to Henry and Li Ming.

* * *

Gabor nodded towards the other room. "Is she back?"

"Yes, she came back a little while ago. We just drank tea. Want some?"

Gabor shook his head.

Babylonia leaned against the sink. "My dad is having an affair."

He stood beside her with his nose in her hair.

"Is that why she's here?"

Babylonia nodded

"He told you that when he called?"

"No, he didn't say a word about it."

She stopped abruptly when Alice came into the kitchen. "I have to pay back a small debt from last night. Be right back."

"Where are you going?"

"Out."

"What do you mean out?"

"Just across the street. I'll be right back."

She left.

"Just out!" Babylonia snapped.

"Who can she owe money to? Here?" Gabor shook his head.

"Unreal," said Babylonia. "You and I know no one in this neighborhood but my mother is now waving to people in the street and has small debts to secret acquaintances. It's totally absurd."

She walked to the window and looked down at the street. Gabor followed.

"Must be somebody at that bar. She was there yesterday."

Gabor looked over at the bar. Before yesterday, he'd never really thought much about it being there. It was so uninteresting that it was completely invisible. Now Alice had made the bar visible, discernible among everything Chinese.

"And the man she slept with sounds very strange," she continued. "Had a head-hunting spear in his bed. Apparently he's Danish."

"Aren't the Danes sort of well-known for being a bit risqué?"

"A head-hunting spear isn't risqué. It's more, like, freaky."

"Or just pretentious. He might take himself a little too seriously," said Gabor.

She turned and stared at him. Patted him on the cheek and felt almost a little tender. He was so boring.

* * *

Outside, Alice found Henry talking to the Chinese baker, Freddy. And Freddy wanted to treat the stylish lady to a bun—the lady that he thought looked like a real movie star, or a lawyer—but she kindly declined. Just wanted to give Henry some money, she said. And she told Henry how someone had grabbed the money, how she'd almost been robbed. And Henry of course didn't want to take her money but she insisted.

"Thank you very much," he said in the finest Smålandian Swedish.

Freddy nodded and went back into his bakery. Alice lingered near Henry. Wanted to stand there and chat with her new friend. Feel that she was part of the street now, a part of all the everyday life that hurried past. No longer that insecure woman in a travel suit who had stood there and almost gotten dirty water from a bucket poured over her feet less than twenty hours ago. She sensed how people were looking at her, curious now that they realized she was acquainted with Henry. And the language! Swedish, Smålandian, with its soft rhythm that sounded so different from the melodious Cantonese.

They stood there and chatted for a while, Alice and Henry, when through the sun's rays she caught sight of a something strange happening down the street.

Although it seemed quite impossible, someone—who very much resembled Charles—was just then being beaten up by two men in suits next to a black limousine.

She squinted.

It *was* Charles who was being beaten up by two men next to a black limousine.

"You see that...?" she exclaimed, and without thinking she rushed down the street.

Henry stared after her. She had rushed off in mid-sentence. But then he shrugged, put out his cigarette and walked across the street into the fabric store.

* * *

Babylonia looked out the window again and saw Henry cross the street and go through the door into his shop. Alice was nowhere to be seen.

She walked back toward the kitchen but stopped in the bedroom and looked around. Perhaps they could redecorate. Get real nightstands. If she didn't move out, of course.

If she did move, how would she want to furnish her new place? A simple futon on the floor. Nothing else. Existence was, after all, so fleeting.

When would she feel that she wanted to get permanent furniture? Or did life slowly snare you and one day—perhaps when you were thirty-five—you woke up with a formal multi-page lease on a place that was way too expensive, forcing you to work long hours in a bank or a slaughterhouse or something, somewhere you had no desire to work. Would she ever find herself living a life like the one she grew up in, she wondered, as she smoothed the wrinkled blanket on the bed.

Would she one day find herself looking around in a house that reminded her of her home in Äppelviken and realize that you can never change who you basically are? Buried, swallowed up by cookie jars, toy bicycles and piles of work you took home.

She picked up Elvis and buried her nose in his black fur. Could you really choose? The realization that she could wind up missing out on all that was even more terrifying. That she could wind up just wandering around here, perpetually young like another Dorian Gray, and never get to experience children, family, career.

She sensed Gabor standing in the doorway looking at her. She looked up and met his gaze.

"What are you thinking, Babi?" he asked.

"About furniture," she replied vaguely. "One may never be able to leave one's past behind."

"I left Hungary and came here."

"But you're still you."

"But if I go back, I will most likely find that I'm no longer who I once was," he said, so annoyingly sensible. "I've changed."

She dropped the cat on the floor. "I'm going down to look for my mother."

* * *

As Alice came rushing up, two big beefy men in their fifties had Charles backed up against a wall and were hitting him a little here and there.

Some youngsters who were playing basketball on the court across the street had paused their game to watch the limousine, the type of car that wasn't the most common of conveyances down here. When this woman came running up, they all stopped playing and stood quiet and mesmerized, staring at what was happening across the street, prepared to run the other way, toward the Manhattan Bridge, at the first sign of trouble. Because you never knew how things would unfold. A big black limousine from which men in suits threw another man out on the sidewalk—a man they then proceeded to beat up—could only mean trouble for any spectator. It was the type of thing that forced you to see things that you should never even pretend to have seen. They should just close their eyes, continue playing as if nothing unusual was taking place across the street. But... they looked at each other... now with this lady running up, things were a little too interesting for them to care about being cautious.

"Stop it, right now," she screamed at the beefy men. "What do you think you're doing?"

The men in suits stopped hitting Charles, turned in surprise and stared at the elegant woman, who had come rushing out of nowhere, as if this were any of her business. Dressed in a turtleneck sweater, beige trousers and brown suede pumps. And holding a wallet in her hand, visibly. Here, in this neighborhood.

"Excuse me, but what did you say?" asked one of the men in surprise.

Charles tried to brush himself off while he stretched, moaned, and straightened out his tie.

Alice stopped—a bit confused now. It was easy to run up and start yelling, but now that she was there, she realized this might not be any of her business.

"Is there something you want? What was it you said?"

"You can't just go around hitting people," she said uncertainly in her best Oxford English.

"But, my dear. We're not hitting anyone. We're only having a little discussion."

Charles turned to her.

"It's okay, Alice. No one's fighting. You misunderstood. Everything's fine. I promise."

The black backseat window rolled down and Amanda's friend Sal stuck his head out. The reptilian eyes sparkled when he saw her.

"Who do we have here? Good afternoon. Are you in the neighborhood again?"

He turned to Charles. "European chick, right?"

Charles nodded.

Sal turned to the thugs. "I think our discussion is done, gentlemen."

He turned to Alice and smiled kindly.

"Don't worry, my dear. Mr. Claessen here is my tenant and we had a small misunderstanding, you see. But it's all cleared up now."

He turned to Charles again. "I'm sure it won't happen again." He leaned forward and continued with a curt smile. "Everything is fine now, my dear. Right?"

As if he wasn't still trying to catch his breath after repeated blows, Charles beckoned with the hand that wasn't holding his stomach.

"Everything's fine, sir. Wonderful, in fact."

Sal turned to Alice again.

"Welcome to this country, sweetheart. You see, you can't fly off the handle in that European sort of way here. If you can't behave calmly, there's a great risk that the authorities will put you on the first plane back home, and you don't want that to happen, now do you?" he nodded sagely. "I understand that things are bad over there in Europe right now. There's a war going on. Again. So be careful, little lady."

He motioned to the men who jumped into the car, waved to the youngsters across the street. The engine started with a soft hum and the car slid along Catherine Street down toward the East River.

Alice turned to Charles. He waved her away with the hand that wasn't holding his stomach.

"It wasn't what it looked like. A bit of fun, mostly. But I need a drink. A really fancy cocktail."

He flagged down a taxi that appeared out of nowhere—like they almost always do—like a magic carpet in *One Thousand and One Nights*.

"Are you coming?"

She hesitated at first, but when he jumped into the cab and left the door open behind him, she got in too.

Across the street, the basketball players said, "Some shit, huh?" in their own local urban slang, gave each other high-fives, of course, and continued playing as if nothing had happened. After all, nothing too remarkable had happened. No one was shot and the police hadn't come. Just an old lady sticking her nose in where it didn't belong.

* * *

Meanwhile, we find Babylonia leaving 120 Catherine Street to look for Alice. An Alice who usually didn't owe money to people in Chinatown, or come home without her stockings, with disheveled just-got-laid hair, the day after a night out on the town. Who should be sitting in her little car on the way to her own life at the university just north of Stockholm, instead of tramping through her daughter's life here.

She took a walk down the street, looked into the different stores. Food stores, the acupuncturist, the fabric store. Everything had been closed and gated when she and Gabor had left for the theater the night before.

Outside the thick wooden door to the bar called BAR, she stopped, hesitated. Looked through the windows, but it was difficult to see anything through the dirty glass. Stood there and thought for a moment. The people she had seen going in and out of that door were mostly old drunks, homeless men. But how to get rid of this feeling of discomfort? This paralyzing feeling that filled her before she stepped through a door, any door, whether it was the door to a swanky boutique where she would undoubtedly be judged by a snooty salesperson, or the door to a closed auditorium where everyone would turn around when she stepped in, or the door to a new job, or a new boyfriend's parents' house, or a cage filled with bored tigers...

Or just the door of a drab bar, in her own neighborhood, full of... well, what?

She braced herself, pushed the door open and stepped inside.

The dark-haired woman she was used to seeing open the gates to the bar was inside. Sweaty, but beautiful in a sensual, almost animal-like way, she stood behind the bar drying glasses. A strand of hair hung down over her eyes.

Two worn-out old men sat next to each other at the bar and stared at her as she stopped at the door. One had marcelled hair and red lipstick, the other a beer belly and a puffy face with traces of a more beautiful self somewhere under all his sad shagginess.

Other than that, it was empty and desolate in there.

Amanda looked up at the new arrival. She blew away the strand of hair that hung down over her eyes and waited for this girl, who she used to see pass by outside the dirty windows on Catherine Street, to say something. She looked frightened. Her breasts bulged under her T-shirt. She seemed completely unaware that it was exceedingly obvious that she didn't wear a bra. So innocent—in this town filled with indulgent debauchery. She wouldn't be wanting a drink at this hour—that's for sure. Although you never know.

She put down the glass and the towel.

"And what can I get you, honey?"

Babylonia looked around again, expecting to see Alice sitting there in the shadows in some hidden corner. The venue smelled of old drunks and unclean bodies. Years of spilled booze marinated the floor and the bar. The smell of cigarette smoke had impregnated the wood-paneled walls where it remained for decades.

"I'm looking for my mother."

Amanda nodded at Bob, the older man with the nice hair and bright red lipstick.

"Other than me, that's the only lady in here."

Babylonia glanced at the man and got a shy Mona Lisa smile back. She turned to the beautiful bartender again. "My mother was in here with you last night. She had locked herself out."

Amanda lit up. "Oh, you mean Alice. Yes, she was here yesterday. So sweet."

And the smile, the warmth in the large dark eyes; the ethereal delicacy that didn't belong here in this ugly bar, that quality that couldn't be described but that shimmered...

It bewitched Babylonia.

"She made it home, I hope?" Amanda continued, oblivious to the effect she was having on her guest. "I lost her."

"Oh yes." And Babylonia felt that it was no longer so important. Now what she mostly wanted was to stay here. Sit and talk to this woman. But first she had to explain.

"The thing is, she's disappeared again."

Amanda frowned. "Disappeared? What do you mean? "

"She went out a while ago and she hasn't come back."

Amanda took out a pack of Marlboros from her apron pocket.

"You sound like you think your mom is mentally retarded…"

"No, she's not. But…"

"Then she probably just took a little walk, dear." Amanda patted Babylonia's hand calmly. Her hand felt rough.

"Don't worry now. She'll be back soon. I'm sure of it."

She offered her a Marlboro. Babylonia took the cigarette mostly so she could touch the woman's hand again. The old man with the marcelled hair leaned forward. His thin hand held a little lighter in the shape of a gun.

"Bang," he said in a squeaky voice when the flame shot out of the barrel of the lighter, and had himself a good laugh.

"Don't go choking now, Bob," said Amanda softly in her dark raspy voice and poured him another drink.

Babylonia took a deep drag and immediately started coughing.

"My mother was just going to run out and pay back some money she owed," she said. "To you, I thought."

Amanda looked affronted.

"She owes no money here, love."

"But, I don't understand. She was here, right? A little while ago."

Amanda shook her head.

"She just ran downstairs to pay someone back. I don't understand…"

"Not me. Maybe she met someone else in this neighborhood last night." She picked up some empty glasses from the two old men.

"That must be it, don't you think?"

"She met a man named Carl, Charles, a Dane." Babylonia almost whispered. "Do you have any regulars named Charles. A bit old-fashioned?"

Amanda nodded towards her customers.

"Everyone here is a bit old-fashioned, as you can see. But I have no regulars named Charles. No Danish regulars at all, actually. Mostly Eastern Europeans, aside from these nice customers." She pointed to Bob and Mel. "These particular two are real natives, if you can say that about someone who isn't an American Indian."

Babylonia glanced at the men who nodded back at her: The one with the fine wavy hair and the other one who mostly looked like someone should comb and shave him and wash his—actually—quite stylish jacket.

"Irish," he said solemnly, raising his glass, "from Lindenhurst." As if that explained everything.

How could she have been afraid to come in here? Why did she allow her imagination to get the better of her, making places off limits just because she hadn't been in them before, as if they were full of aliens, as if facing the unfamiliar was impossible? As if the move from Äppelviken to New York had been so enormous that it sufficed. Once in the big city, she stuck to what she knew: her job, her theater and her Gabor, she didn't really long for more. Had instead wanted to create a little world of peace and security here in the great chaos.

And she'd succeeded.

But now she had ventured into this bar, not a student hangout, or a comprehensible, trendy bar, but a small trashy, unknown bar—a place where you could run into something, even if that *something*, that danger, was so vague that she couldn't put it into words. And what was so threatening about a waitress who had the biggest eyes she had ever seen in real life and two old gentlemen who perhaps had a story to tell?

Mesmerized, she stared first at the beautiful woman, and then at the two other customers. Because you might turn into one of these worn-out men if you hung out here. Could easily happen to her if she stayed on Catherine Street with Gabor and they continued walking around in the same circles and let these circles get smaller and smaller while the city grew bigger and bigger around them. Until, finally, she'd be doing nothing other than coming down here to the bar from her apartment every day, letting the walk to the bar called BAR and the time she spent there become like a job, a full-time job...

It felt—easy!

She was suddenly terrified that the vision of herself as a regular here was feeling so easy, so pleasant... so possible.

Behind her, she felt the air as the door opened and the smell of Catherine Street spilled in—or perhaps it was the familiar smell of something else. She turned around and there stood Gabor in the doorway with his Roots backpack, frowning, surprised to see a lit cigarette in her hand.

She motioned for him to come in. Thought reluctantly that his presence here made her feel secure, so that the bar couldn't swallow her up. Put a spell on her.

And when Amanda turned to Gabor with the same warmth she always had for all her customers and said, "What'll it be?" Babylonia thought it was completely incomprehensible that a person could look like she really cared about what a guy like Gabor wanted to order in this, her shabby bar. Inconceivable that this beautiful creature really cared about whether the old guys were okay or that she really cared about making sure that she, Babylonia, didn't feel uncomfortable on the uncomfortable bar stool. The woman radiated goodness, plain and simple.

It was very strange.

Amanda looked intently at Gabor again and repeated, "What'll it be?" As if she really cared about whether he would order beer or whiskey or a small Calvados.

Gabor stepped up to the bar and took Babylonia's hand. Turned to Amanda and replied that he probably just wanted the check so that they could leave.

Preferably now.

But now Babylonia wanted to stay. Wanted to continue talking with Amanda. Wanted to get clarity. Though she wasn't sure about what. She held on tightly to the glass of beer Amanda put in front of her. Reluctantly, Gabor sat down on the bar stool next to her.

"Your father called," he said.

"Again. Oh, God. I hope he isn't on his way here."

Because now, she had changed her mind. Didn't want her father to come here and straighten things out. Began to realize that perhaps it wasn't possible to straighten anything out for her parents. And it really was none of her concern.

"He's here," said Gabor laconically.

"Here!"

"The Burns Hotel up by the Empire State Building."

"He's where?" It took a while for this to sink in. She breathed heavily and turned straight toward him. "But why? That's not a very nice place."

"Do you think he should sleep on the vinyl couch too?"

"No. Of course not."

Silence again and Amanda looked amiably at Gabor while she waited for his order—which never came.

"He mumbled something about some Mister Man who took his wallet," said Gabor finally. "Will call us back after he's done with his Swedish bank."

"His bank."

"Yes, calling the bank."

"But… Wait? Do you mean to say he was mugged?"

Babylonia put her glass down with a bang on the bar and turned to him. Now completely appalled. Her father Göran was here—and on top of it all, he'd been mugged.

Gabor twisted a finger around one of his long ringlets as he always did when he was confused and had no cigarettes. Asking Amanda for a cigarette was too complicated.

"I didn't really understand," he said. "Something about helping him with his luggage and… no, I didn't understand. Some Mister Man carrying bags. Sounds preposterous."

He sighed and looked around.

At the far end of the bar there was a simple toilet where Pavel had already been standing for a minute, in the dark by the toilet door gazing at the new arrivals. When he saw that Gabor saw him standing there, he sauntered out into the light and sat down ceremoniously, scraping the bar stool along the floor, and rapped on the bar.

"A Pilsner Urquell here, thank you," he said clearly, wouldn't settle for anything else this time.

He tapped rhythmically on the bar and totally unexpectedly and almost bluntly, began singing a little song to himself in a powerful bass voice, slightly off-key and in a language that might have been Russian—and that no one else understood. Except perhaps Gabor.

Amanda poured two Millers on draft for Gabor and Pavel.

"My treat," she said. "Where were we? Alice, yes. Do you know where she went yesterday, Pavel?"

17

A bit uptown, pretty close to the Empire State Building, in an elegant and desolate cocktail bar in a classic New York hotel in the best
Art Deco style, Alice and Charles were being served extra stiff dry
martinis by a taciturn bartender. The glasses were lightly iced. A
shiny olive lay like a promise of something a little more astringent
in the clear pure liquid. Charles took the check and searched his
pockets, looking embarrassed at the few coins and crumpled bills he
found.

Alice took out her wallet. For a moment, Charles looked uncomfortable—but not for a very long moment.

"Embarrassing," he lifted his glass. "But thanks and cheers."

She took a small sip of her drink while she gave her credit card to
the waiter. Felt naked without her handbag, but in this cool air-
conditioned place with its round furniture in clean lines she
nevertheless felt quite at home.

She was now on her second day of consuming alcohol as early as
lunchtime. On the other hand, this felt like a very special occasion.
She had never had to break up a fight between adults before. And
she thought that it was actually kind of wonderful to sit in a bar in
the middle of the day drinking a dry martini. So unlike the old
Alice.

She looked around. Farther down the bar sat a little, curly Irish-looking man, a James Cagney type from the thirties, as if he had traveled through time and had landed in this bar, wearing a pin-stripe suit with a clock hanging out of his pocket. He was reading a newspaper and contentedly sipping a large whiskey.

Charles sat on the bar stool next to her, looking down into his glass, a thoughtful frown between his eyebrows. She tapped him on the thigh.

"Now you must try to explain to me why your landlord beats up his tenants."

Charles looked up and started fidgeting with his cigarette paraphernalia.

"You're exaggerating. We were discussing a problem I had with the private club next door to my apartment." Charles took a big gulp again, lifted the glass to the light. "Excellent. I needed this."

"But I saw that you were doing more than just discussing."

"He's not just anyone, my landlord." He gave her an urgent look to see if she understood. She looked at him, politely quizzical.

"Well?"

"He thought I had let the police wire my apartment so they could eavesdrop on his club."

"And why would they want to do that?"

"They had asked me to but I said no, of course."

"The police asked if they could put eavesdropping equipment in your living room?"

He nodded.

"And you said no...?"

"Yes, I value my health, so to speak."

Alice pondered this for a moment then said forcibly, "Absurd!"

She sat quietly for a while and then shook her head.

"You're kidding, right? These things only happen in the old

Soviet Union... or with the Mafia."

He said nothing.

She sipped her drink.

"I should really go to work now," he said after a moment. But nothing more was said, he just remained seated there on his bar stool next to her.

Alice looked around again. Farther down the bar they had now been joined by a middle-aged couple in gaudy evening clothes. They sat at a small table, resolute and quiet, while the bartender served them a bottle of champagne. Bollinger. Vintage, she noticed. The woman leafed through a theater program. Her hair looked stiff and newly styled. Her dress was a little too tight across the chest. The man poked at the lapel of his tuxedo. Uncomfortable in his attire. Imprisoned like a clumsy dressed-up elephant, he looked around, restless. Looked at the clock, downed his champagne and glared longingly at James Cagney's soft yellow whiskey. He lit a cigar and exhaled a huge cloud of smoke that drifted over toward them. Alice coughed before the smoke had even reached them. Charles waved away the smoke symbolically with his hand, leaned over and took her hand in his.

"Look, I'm going to skip work. Can't go to the office now. It's been a little too much today, don't you agree?"

"Well," she said softly. "Yes, maybe."

Avoiding eye contact, and with an embarrassed glint in his eyes he suddenly blurted out, "Can't we go back to my place and continue where we left off this morning?"

He smiled, and when she didn't respond immediately his smile became uncertain.

She said nothing. Sat quietly. Wanted to think.

He was coming on to her. Very strange.

She wanted to think about what she felt before she replied,

wanted to think about whether she felt anything at all. Looked over at the couple. Watched as the woman turned to the man. Hissed something at him, short and irritated. The man looked at the clock again and snapped gloomily back at her and an oppressive, massive silence descended between them. The woman grasped the Playbill tightly as if it were a life preserver, while he poured himself some more champagne.

Alice turned to Charles and he winked conspiratorially at her. Flirtatiously. And the wink, it really was very silly, she thought. And his bushy sideburns looked like they were glued onto his lean cheeks—they weren't something she would have chosen or wanted. But what *would* she have wished for? If she were about to experiment with a whole new lifestyle, a lifestyle in which she intervened in fights outside shiny limousines? Having come this far in her metamorphosis, why wouldn't she consider going back to this Danish man's place and letting him seduce her? Again.

She leaned back in her chair. Ate her olive and turned toward him.

"Shall we take a taxi?" She replied before she changed her mind.

And it was totally intoxicating, this simply acting on impulse rather than following a detailed plan.

He held her hand more tightly. They finished their drinks quickly and glided like two royals out through the lobby to a waiting taxi. A yellow Chevrolet Caprice.

That was there, parked out front, waiting.

Of course.

* * *

Down at the bar called BAR on Catherine Street in Chinatown, Amanda's thick eyebrows were frowning at Pavel who still just sat there drumming his fingers on the bar.

"But did you see what happened to her? Where she went?"

Pavel shook his head and gave them an absent smile. Like Stan Laurel, the corners of his mouth went up but the smile never reached further than that.

Babylonia wished she could get a clear picture of how her mother had ended up in an underground nightclub with this man, who was wearing a too small jacket, was unshaven, with a slightly crazed look in his eyes.

"She said a man from Yugoslavia took her to a small gambling joint," Babylonia said softly. "A small gambling club filled with gangsters."

Amanda threw a sharp glance at Pavel again.

"Pavel!"

He interrupted her quickly. "Yeah, I mean… sure!" He took a long drag on his cigarette. "I saw her there. Sure I did. With a Danish guy." He nodded as if this explained everything. "And I saw her a little while ago, too," he continued after another puff on the cigarette that was now as near its butt as a cigarette could be. "I saw her on Mulberry Street with that Dane. A guy with connections."

"With what?"

"*Connections, contacts.* I see him everywhere, all the time."

"What kind of contacts?"

Pavel fidgeted.

"Shady guys… well, you know…"

"Was this Danish man with my mother?"

Pavel looked from Babylonia to Amanda, confused.

"Who's her mother?"

"Get with the program, Pavel" said Amanda and patted Babylonia on the hand. "Don't worry honey. We'll find her for you."

Gabor stood up abruptly and pointed at Pavel.

"You're from Yugoslavia!"

Pavel turned on his stool and looked at Gabor slit-eyed.

"And who are you? What right do you have to open your mouth?" Gabor gathered his forces.

"You're deranged. Tell us what you've done with her."

"Me? I see to my own affairs. Are you dim, or what? Didn't you hear what I said? Moron!"

"Moron?" Gabor fell silent and looked as if the word moron had been created just for him.

Pavel drank his Miller and slammed the glass down on the bar; he did not want to continue this discussion.

Amanda sighed and gave Pavel a stern look.

"Stop bickering! We have to focus on finding her mother. If you're going to engage in some ridiculous cock fight, you can just get out of here."

Babylonia wanted to just drink up and leave. Her father in New York, mugged—checked into a tourist hotel in dreary midtown. And Alice—she had not only disappeared, but was living a life of her own that she's told her daughter nothing about. She had appeared on Catherine Street less than a day ago and was already behaving as if she had lived here her entire life. Had her own friends. Was visible. Noticed on the street by people who belonged in the neighborhood. Waved to Chinese people on the street who didn't even notice her, Babylonia, when she bought milk in the same shop she went into every single day. But Alice, well, she had just stepped into this, her world, and behaved as if she belonged here.

Pavel dug in his pockets and came up with a couple of bills and was now finally buying a bottle of Pilsner Urquell. He turned to Babylonia—and ignored Gabor.

"Hey, if Alice is really your mother, which I find hard to believe, let me just say that she's the type of person who does just fine no matter what the situation. She has a sort of safety net of innocence, you know what I mean?"

He spread out his arms and almost poked Gabor in the eye with his cigarette.

"A safety net of what?"

"Bullshit," murmured Gabor.

Pavel's feathers got ruffled again.

"Bullshit?" He wagged his finger. "YOU are bullshit, the whole of you..."

Amanda suddenly slammed her fist down on the bar causing a glass to overturn.

"Knock it off. Stop it. This is New York City, you buffoons. There's room for everyone. This is a place of business. Basta! Good lord!"

Bob stood up and approached the group, stood there with a long, slender, brown cigarette in a mother-of-pearl holder, patted his fine hair, as if he wanted them to note that it was almost newly styled.

He leaned forward and said warmly, "I was once in Yugoslavia. The Balkan Peninsula, so beautiful!" He raised his glass. "Cheers."

Pavel toasted solemnly. Amanda patted Babylonia's hand.

"It'll all turn out okay, you'll see, honey. You just have to be kind. That's my motto. You just have to be kind."

* * *

Meanwhile, a somewhat more composed Göran sat with a whiskey in his hand at the same hotel that Alice had just left. He called the answering machine on Catherine Street.

In the apartment, Elvis crouched smoothly over the answering machine. It made such interesting clicks every time someone called. Without much effort, he did what he usually does...slowly and pleasurably knocked the receiver off the hook with his paw. Göran heard someone pick up the phone on the other end.

"Hello, hello." He swore irritably over the fact that no one on the other end of the line said anything. "Hello. Alice, is that you? Answer me goddammit!"

Elvis sat beside the receiver and licked his paw. Sensuously, between his claws. He was extremely pleased with himself.

* * *

Gabor unlocked his bicycle. Muttered as he stood bent over the lock. "The past 24 hours have been a bit too much for me. I'm going to the library now." He stood up, put the key in his pocket and stared up the street.

"Right now? Is that such a good idea?" she said, and felt taken aback that he was leaving. Now.

He continued to avoid looking at her and she got a queasy feeling in her stomach, something was slipping away from her.

"Your father will be calling any moment now. So you'd best go up to the apartment and wait for his call. And while you're at it, I wish that you'd give some serious thought to what you want," he continued. "We can't continue like this. It doesn't feel right. Either we're together or we're not."

She stood quietly and watched as he fastened his backpack to his bike rack.

"See ya." He mounted the bike and stared gloomily in front of him.

She walked over and touched his arm, but he pushed her hand away and turned gravely to her again.

"Either you're here when I come back because you want to be with me, or if that's not what you want, then I want you to check into a hotel with your mom or your dad or both. I don't care!"

Without even giving her a light kiss, the way he usually did, he rode away—and she stood there in the street and wondered how she could suddenly feel so alone. Not in the least bit liberated and strong with a world of possibilities before her.

She looked through the window into the bar where she caught a glimpse of Amanda, but she couldn't go in there again. No way.

Instead, she walked slowly back to their building.

18

In the dim afternoon light in Charles's ground-floor apartment, they lay naked next to each other on clean sheets decorated in large patterns and made of synthetic materials. He had first been embarrassed by them. Didn't want to change the bed into his only clean sheets. But Alice, who has the nose of a bloodhound when it comes to dirty sheets, had insisted on clean bedding.

As they lay there naked, she thought how strange it was that she'd become accustomed to his body so quickly. This stranger's body. Her hand stroked his swollen cock, the glans that was both similar to and different from others she'd touched. He breathed in and leaned over her, kissed her deeply and long. She closed her eyes and thought for a brief second of Göran, but the image was difficult to capture, as if his contours had become diffuse, a fuzzy image. She dismissed the image, opened her eyes and looked up at the man she was now in bed with, in a small apartment on Mulberry Street—in another continent than her marriage bed in Äppelviken.

The light in the apartment on the other side of the small dark concrete courtyard just went on. The beam of light was like a ribbon over her belly, where his head with the now disheveled sideburns worked its way down to the place between her legs. He didn't look like anyone she'd ever let get there, so close, in the past—with those hilarious sideburns, lion tattoo and his slicked down hair. Nevertheless, there he lay between her legs and she thought that she never wanted to travel back in time and go back to being that other Alice again, the one who worked at the university and lived in a house in Äppelviken.

Instead she closed her eyes and, despite her guilty conscience, allowed herself to enjoy and give in to being pleasured. And when he entered her, she was completely in the moment, didn't think about the dry cleaning or work or television or the car or anything else that can distract you from making love.

And he looked down at her face and her closed eyes and felt that he might, in that very moment, be witnessing something a little bit miraculous.

* * *

Babylonia walked slowly up the many stairs, heard a door open. Someone stood still behind it and when he became aware that she was climbing the stairs, closed it again. The apartments she passed were completely silent, as if she lived in a house that wasn't real. You could hear the neighbors sometimes, knew they existed. Could hear the rooster, smell the sour odor of cat pee. But that was it.

She opened the door to their apartment. All the complicated locks. The regular lock up top, the big lock at the bottom—and the old police lock with an iron rod that was anchored in a worn groove in the floor. It always gave her trouble. And all this worn stuff: the impractical temporary solutions for locks and plugs, all the worn bathroom cabinets, moldings, old gas stoves which were like time bombs inside the dilapidated apartments—just standing there waiting to explode at any moment—all the stuff that had seemed so charming in its ramshackle dangerousness when she first moved in, was now starting to feel tiresome.

Inside, she found the phone off the hook. Elvis and Loser were lying at opposite ends of the couch, asleep. She hung up the receiver and crawled out on the fire escape, sat down, closed her eyes and held her breath.

She hadn't made any serious impact on the universe. Would anyone even notice if she ceased to exist? If she stopped breathing. The only thing that would be left of her was the air that had been in her lungs which she now slowly exhaled.

She wanted to start over.

Reinvent herself.

Make a fresh start.

What was she doing here? She didn't belong here. She longed for the smell of green grass, clean fresh rain, clover, the taste of salt licorice. Swedish newspapers and the television programs of her youth.

But now she was sitting here on the worn fire escape, looking down at the dirty garbage, at strangers passing by. She missed trees, missed that indescribable something. The sense of the pure, the unadorned, the predictable and straightforward.

Home. The thought of what home ought to be both attracted and frightened her.

Down on the street, people were bringing vegetables indoors. The sky was icy blue above the roofs. The blue was mixed with something yellow from pollution. Across the street women sat and sewed at their small sewing machines, even though it was Friday night and everyone else in town was getting ready to enjoy what the city offered, be it Shakespeare in the Park, marathon techno dancing, sex, all kinds of religion, or simply an ordinary Friday at home with the family, in a slightly messy apartment filled with empty Chinese takeout cartons, somewhere hundreds of feet above the ground

But the women across the street, they just sat there and sewed, heads bent over their sewing machines.

How had it come to this? How had she ever been able to find this misery beautiful? There was no justice or beauty in this. She'd been tricked. Suckered in. And she'd never felt so alone. She wanted to go home. But what was home now? She wanted to be outdoors, walk in the woods, see the ocean. But the only forest available here was Central Park. And the ocean, that was there beyond Brooklyn, was over an hour's rattling subway ride away. Everything was just too big. And all of this just enhanced the new sense of desolation that was beginning to overpower her. It was as if her mother Alice had shined a huge spotlight on her life. As if her presence had made it clear how estranged she felt here.

Down at the bar called BAR, the heavy wooden door opened and the beautiful woman, whose name Babylonia didn't yet know was Amanda, came out. With a graceful gesture she swept back the bangs that had fallen down over her eyes. Her wide thin coat blew open to reveal a dress so short that it looked more like a sweater. She looked around and began walking briskly in her laced thigh-high boots down the street towards 120 Catherine Street.

Babylonia stood up abruptly and ran through the apartment. The cats lifted their heads lazily and looked at her. She stopped at the front door and stood, petrified, staring at the intercom which, after five long seconds, gave off a sharp signal. She stared at all those little gray plastic buttons that you were supposed to press to let someone in—but she simply couldn't bring herself to lift her hand.

When the intercom fell silent, she made her way back to the window and peered down at Amanda who was standing down there looking around. She rushed back to the kitchen again, pressed the intercom talk button but didn't make a sound. Instead, she had trouble breathing and leaned against the wall.

When the phone rang, she spun around and accidentally knocked over a glass sending it crashing to the floor. She leaned against the kitchen counter and slowly sank into a sitting position amid the shattered glass, ignoring the ringing phone. Just sat there waiting for it to stop.

19

A cool breeze blew in from the Atlantic, gained momentum over Brooklyn, continued across the East River, caressed the rooftops in Chinatown and caused the first leaves that had fallen from a tree on Mulberry Street to twirl around the garbage in the gutter. Perhaps it would be cooler tomorrow. It was now completely dark. As dark it can be on a street in a big city.

Outside Charles's building, the super was sitting in his undershirt on a folding chair. As the evening breeze picked up, he put on a worn Yankee sweatshirt. He had the *New York Post* in his hand and was carefully studying the evening's lineup at Belmont. He longed for the end of the month when racing season would properly begin. He wondered if investing in that horse had really been a good idea, although he would never admit that he had any second thoughts about this to his wife, who was sitting there beside him—on a similar folding chair. She had a shawl over her shoulders and was knitting a baby sweater. The long silver needles glistened in the glow of the street lights. The sweater would soon be done. Fuzzy pink.

The neighbor, one Lucia Palermo who'd grown up in the neighborhood, hung out the window adjacent to the door. Her large breasts rested on the windowsill. Long white hair lay in a thick braid over her shoulder. She held a long and lively monologue about the eating habits of her new son-in-law, a Russian.

"No one in my family has ever married a Russian before. He's not even Catholic. Everything they eat is pickled. Nothing fresh. You can tell by just looking at them."

She stopped abruptly when the door opened and Alice and Charles stepped out.

"Everything okay, Claessen?" asked the super and lowered the newspaper.

"A lady friend, I see," said the super's wife. She looked Alice up and down and gave Lucia Palermo with the thick braid a meaningful glance. "A relative, perhaps?" she cocked her head. "How nice."

"Nice!" the other one echoed in agreement.

Alice held out her hand and the super's wife took it with a glance at her husband. Allowed her to touch only the outermost tips of her fingers. After having introduced herself as Mrs. Tancredi, she looked over at her friend again. "A relative, perhaps?" she repeated.

Alice shook her head. Amused, but still with an embarrassed sense of nakedness before these women. Aware that her hair was disheveled, that her skin was still rosy from what had just taken place up there in his little gray apartment. She was sticky, moist, fragrant. Felt like a sensual animal instead of the composed academic that she actually was in her real life.

"May I offer you a little cookie dear?" Lucia Palermo asked and leaned out of the window. "It's almond. From a family recipe."

She held out a small biscuit in her hand. Alice didn't dare refuse and felt compelled to stick the little cookie, moist from sweaty palms, into her mouth while the woman nodded encouragingly.

Meanwhile, Charles lit a cigarette and then asked Mr. Tancredi to see to his oven door which would not close properly. They got embroiled in a conversation about furnaces, fireplaces, gas pipes, radiators. Alice stood silently beside them, avoided making eye contact with the ladies, although she could sense them exchanging meaningful glances. She sucked in the evening air through her teeth to remove the taste of the cookie. She was sleepy and hungry for real food, and maybe a little worried that she hadn't gotten a hold of Babylonia to let her know where she was.

She had to pick up her bag soon; should check into a hotel, call work, fax her husband—no, not fax him. But she should really get in touch with Sweden. She had students who expected to meet with her—tomorrow. The dean was waiting for her draft on liability and behavior patterns. But having the courage to drop everything, to be totally irresponsible, careless, to simply vanish— these were surprisingly pleasant feelings. Living with a wallet as her only luggage, without plans. It was like leaning back against a comfortable down pillow when you're sick and knowing that you can let go of all responsibility. Take time off from yourself. TAKE TIME OFF FROM YOURSELF! You weren't allowed to do that. It was as if you wove an invisible net around yourself through the years until it was too late and you were completely entangled in calendars, seasons, academic planning, preserving lingonberries, mushroom picking and the car-needs-to-be-serviced responsibilities.

It was now—if only for a short while—that she had a chance to try a completely different version of herself. Like changing to a new detergent or perfume. To be a woman who slept with tattooed men in small cluttered urban apartments, eat dinner at any time of the day or night and not worry that she didn't have a set of clean clothes or a toothbrush and skin cream available. To believe that it would all work out anyway—somehow.

Charles stood beside her and chatted with his super, who replied in his strong New York accent. Pronounced all soft "th" sounds like a hard d or t. She shaped her silent lips and mimicked the sound. Dared to pretend that she was someone else. Someone with a different kind of life.

And the Italian ladies were no longer particularly interested in her. The one in the window was complaining about something, and the other one commiserated—it sounded like something as mundane as the presence of mice or the price of coffee. And Alice just stood there on the outskirts of the conversation, an altogether different type of woman, the type who slept with men she barely knew—in the middle of the afternoon.

The city around her smelled so indefinably delightful. A woman in a window high above them was laughing, the exhilarating sound of hip-hop pounded from a passing car, the operatic voice down the street was practicing scales again. Next to her, a family was walking into the building, everyone greeted each other and there was laughter at a screaming tired two year old in her father's arms. Someone went skateboarding down the street, a couple walked past entwined, constantly kissing—and a black limousine parked across the street.

Sal climbed out of the car accompanied by two gentlemen in suits. They slipped quickly into position, one diagonally behind Sal and the other beside him. When Sal caught sight of Alice, his face lit up and he crossed the street, followed by the other two keeping an eye out in every direction.

"Well, good evening. Very nice to see you in our neighborhood, again. Incredible, isn't it?" He stopped and took Alice's hand and held it a moment in his. A hairy, slightly sweaty hand, a wide wedding ring pinching his thick ring finger.

"As always, a pleasure to see you, sir," said Charles, with a somewhat unsteady voice Alice thought.

Sal turned his attention from Alice, nodded toward the neighbors standing outside the front door and patted Charles amicably on the back.

"Everything all right?" He repeated the question to the others and everyone mumbled an affirmative answer.

High above them, the opera singer was standing at his window, now silent, studying what was happening on the street. How Sal turned toward the couple with his hand firmly holding the woman's fingers again.

"And where are you youngsters off to then?"

"To have some dinner," replied Charles. "At one of the places down the street."

"So nice. Really." Sal nodded towards Alice and winked conspiratorially. "Our street has quite the European atmosphere that I'm sure will suit the little lady. Good wine, checkered tablecloths, candlelight. You'll feel right at home, sweetheart."

He turned to Charles and added, "But not just any place, right? Some of *those* joints are awful tourist traps. I would love to be of help, if I may."

Without waiting for an answer, he turned to one of his beefy lackeys.

"Go with them down to Cucina Carmela and make sure they get a nice table without having to wait. You know, the usual... or wait a second..."

He turned now to Alice again with a smile and a somewhat insistent look in his eyes. "It's still early, my dear. I would very much like to offer you an aperitif first. What do you say?" A solicitous nod towards Charles. "This way. Follow me."

But Alice had no desire to have an aperitif with this man. The magical atmosphere was about to crumble. She didn't want it disrupted yet. Wanted so desperately to remain the moist, erotic, euphoric Alice. The one who wandered around in a strange city with bachelors she hardly knew who made love to her on flowery synthetic sheets.

"But that's really not necessary," she interrupted Sal quickly.

He turned in the doorway of the place next to Charles's building and raised his eyebrows, amused.

"But… a little aperitif. I won't accept no for an answer. It isn't every day we have ladies from good old Europe visiting."

The opera singer, who suffered from a certain lust for sensational melodrama, nodded to himself up there at his window and resumed practicing his scales. "This isn't going to end well," he thought excitedly with the same feeling that used to spread across his diaphragm at the end of the second act. "Not well at all."

And the Italian ladies, who avoided looking at Alice as she was being pulled into the place next door, now looked up at the window where the singing got louder, shaking their heads and sighing. While the super took the opportunity to immerse himself once again in the horse racing columns.

Everything happened so quickly that Alice couldn't continue to protest. She was pulled through a door, found herself in a narrow passage leading into what appeared to be a former workshop. Maybe an old stable? She could see traces of hooks and tools on the walls.

A couple of older men sat puffing cigars, bent over an ongoing chess game. It smelled of cigarettes and pungent men's colognes whose various sickening essences clashed with each other in the small room and mixed with a stuffy scent she didn't recognize. Thick. Filled with… uneasiness. Farther into the room, at a shiny black glass bar, a bald bartender immediately put down his newspaper when he saw who had walked through the door. Sal greeted the men in the room amicably and nodded to the bartender. "Send up a bottle of our best Chianti."

Charles was holding Alice's hand tightly as they walked up a narrow spiral metal staircase leading to an upper level.

A soft green wall-to-wall carpet covered the floor, even the kitchen area where a luxurious AGA stove was enthroned just above the stairs. She turned to Charles to point out the stove, "A Swedish AGA stove... *here*..." but he avoided her gaze and focused instead on Sal who stood in the middle of the room working a remote control to adjust the room's lighting.

The windows were covered by thick, poppy red velvet curtains. A huge sofa and a glass coffee table took up the front of the room. A hand mirror and a razor lay on the table beside an ornate candle holder. The rest of the room was dominated by a large tub in the form of a giant wooden barrel: a cannibal stewpot.

"Here, you see," said Sal as he took her hand and pulled her toward the tub. "Here, you can take a relaxing bath in a Jacuzzi. Doesn't that sound nice?"

"Nice, indeed," echoed Charles behind her.

Sal turned on the water which trickled down into the tub from a faucet shaped like a dolphin's mouth.

"The tub is custom-made. In pine. Direct from Colorado. Totally unique. Isn't it beautiful? The shape and height of the sides are designed so that you can bathe in it without having to feel embarrassed when there are other people in the room. They're supposed to be the rage in Japan." He smiled and put his arm around her shoulders. "If you want to try it out, we have some nice bathrobes imported from Milan. The best terry cloth on the market. What do you say? "

Charles nudged her softly. "That sounds nice, doesn't it?" she heard him say. And she turned abruptly to see if he was serious, but he coughed nervously and slid over to the couch where he sat down and took out his pack of cigarettes.

The wine was now opened and poured into small crystal glasses that Alice noted were more suitable for liqueur than for a full-bodied Chianti. She took a glass, grateful that so little wine fit into it—tried to catch Charles's gaze. But he avoided looking at her while he lit another cigarette from the previous butt. The man who accompanied them to the upper level remained discreetly in the background, while Sal now went over to the wardrobe and took out a soft terry cloth robe. He handed it to Alice, allowing his finger to caress her hand lightly, and whispered in a deep voice, "Go ahead. You can change in there." He pointed to a closed door next to the AGA stove.

Charles coughed violently and abruptly stood up. "I have to..."

"There," said Sal and pointed to a door further away in the room.

Charles disappeared into the bathroom and Alice just stood there with her glass and the terry cloth robe. Tried to understand what was happening. She was a mentor to young people. How had *she* ended up here? Everything had happened so terribly quickly. One minute they had been standing on the street in a quiet neighborhood on their way to a restaurant. And a second later, she was sitting in something akin to a brothel. This kind of thing didn't happen to her, Alice Berglund, tenured professor at the university. She was so very, very tired. This simply couldn't be real.

She sat down on the sofa, leaned back, trapped in a dream which had been woven like a sticky fuzzy cobweb around her. Sal was moving along the edge of the cobweb, Charles was somewhere far off, passive, not involved.

The sofa felt soft, as if it had swallowed her. The soft stuffing and low height made her feel like a child. She raised her glass of wine to her lips. Looked down at it, smelled it. Knew that if she tasted the plum red liquid she was lost. She stood up. But the sticky cobwebs held on to her and she just stood immobile by the couch and stared at Sal who had changed into a silver striped bathrobe.

He felt the water in the tub while he quietly watched her.

"Mmm. Come on. Go and change now." He came closer, leaned into her, patting her gently on the cheek.

"Charles usually likes it here. The others will soon be here too. Relax now, sweetheart. Would you perhaps like a line—to perk you up, I mean?"

She felt his eyes wandering down to her cleavage. Close. And her passivity gave way to anger, panic began to rise inside her. A line of what? What others? At last she came to life. Got her bearings.

"I think I'll go now. Thank you for the wine." She put down the nearly full glass. "You can tell Charles that I went home. My daughter is waiting for me."

She started walking towards the stairs but Sal caught up with her and put his arm around her. "Take it easy now. No one wants to hurt you. I'm going to take a bath and you drink up the good Chianti. I import it myself."

Without answering she tore herself free from his arm and started down the stairs. It was quiet behind her. She heard someone clearing his throat uncomfortably. "Frigid bitch," it sounded like.

And she heard the other man laugh.

As she hurried down the spiral staircase, she tripped and caught her heel on one of the narrow steps. She pulled her shoe free, causing an ugly tear in the suede. On the lower level, everyone sat petrified and stared up at her as she came down the stairs with the shoe in her hand. The mixture of smells made it hard to breathe. What was that stench? Her heart was pounding. She had to get out. Turned the door handle but the door wouldn't open. She pushed it, jerked the large steel beam that covered the door like a slat. But nothing happened. Turned around, but now everyone was looking down at their chess game—as if she weren't there.

Perhaps she didn't understand the locking mechanism, she thought, now back to her objective self. Wanted to be the usual

Alice and not this woman with a shoe in her hand, who was locked in a room that smelled of... fear. She felt the perspiration on her neck, wiped her forehead. Was completely drenched in sweat.

One of the gentlemen who had been in the car with Sal earlier, stared at her as he quietly opened the door. Did not step aside. But now she was filled with pure rage and pushed him backwards. Could feel something hard under his jacket.

Politely, he held the door open. "Nothing to be afraid of, Madame." He smiled cordially and slinked back into the dimness of the room she'd just left.

Outside, everything was normal, as if the room behind the discreet door didn't exist. The Italian wives had retired. The super sat alone. He looked silently at her with a nondescript expression on his face. He just looked at her without saying a word. A blank look under heavy eyelids.

She stopped, leaned against the wall, wiped her forehead and neck. Her turtleneck sweater stuck to her breasts. Why was she wearing a synthetic bra? She gasped. Maybe she was stupid to just rush away like that. Allowed herself to get scared, gotten the heel of her shoe stuck.

From somewhere high up, you could hear the clatter of pots and a screaming child. A bellowing fire truck drove past on Lafayette Street. The opera singer paused in the middle of a phrase and stood staring at her. But of that, Alice was quite unaware.

She put on her shoe and breathed in the urban air which, despite its exhaust fumes and the humid September heat, felt like fresh mountain air compared to the sickening feeling that hovered like toxic gas on the other side of the door.

She rubbed her eyes. And felt that she had lost her bearings. Where was Chinatown? What was north and what was south? Now that she really needed a taxi the magic didn't work anymore. No car appeared like a magic carpet.

The street was deserted and the super looked pointedly down at his newspaper.

Then, Charles was standing next to her again. Said nothing. Just took her hand.

She looked at him, drew back her hand, took a breath, and tried to take in who he was. This Danish man. Who was he really? And how had she ended up here altogether?

"Sorry," he whispered. "Now let's go and eat."

The super looked up briefly as they started walking down the street.

Almost unnoticed, Sal's burly employee had slipped out the door and begun walking close behind them down the street.

Alice walked silently beside Charles, with Sal's lackey following close behind, wondering whether she had overreacted. No one could have forced her to jump into a large tub with a stranger. And it was just a Jacuzzi. A very ordinary hot tub.

"He said you were a regular there." She said it quietly, perhaps not even out loud. But he answered immediately.

"No. I'm not."

"Microphones in the walls!"

"Believe me."

He stopped and looked her straight in the eyes seriously.

"Alice. I go my own way. I'm not a businessman, like them."

"Businessman?"

"Call it what you want."

They continued, silent for a few moments.

"Alice, I don't think it's wise to turn down an invitation from someone like Sal," Charles said at last. "It was stupid of us to go upstairs. But let's go and eat at his restaurant, and I'll tell you how I ended up in that apartment. It's a pretty ordinary story. A coincidence. His guy here will make sure that we get the best service in the restaurant. We'll get a very nice table, maybe even for free."

"He wanted me to take a bath with him in a cauldron." She began to roar with laughter. But the laughter stopped as suddenly as it had started.

Charles looked at her with concern in his eyes, as if he were expecting just about anything from her right now.

"Sal comes from humble beginnings and has become a very wealthy man. He's proud of his club. And now he wants to help us get a nice table and good service. Why can't we just accept his offer and be happy?"

She glanced back toward the man who was tailing them. He smiled and saluted. It should have made her laugh again, but she just felt provoked.

"It's not right to go around beating people up like that."

"But Alice, honey. Calm down." Charles lowered his voice. "This is not Stockholm or Aarhus. I am, all in all, quite satisfied with my arrangement with him. I have an apartment in lower Manhattan for a cheap rent in a building where I barely need to lock my door. No one—and I mean no one—would ever dream of committing burglary in Little Italy. I love living here."

"Even if you have a good deal, the whole thing is completely absurd." She shook her head and pulled her arm away. "Unacceptable."

"But please… calm down."

She stopped dead.

"No, I won't."

Charles sighed—heavily.

The man, having now caught up with them, stopped. Politely and a little sleepily, he stood and listened to the amusing guttural

Swedish that made everything this rigid woman said sound like she was joking.

Without waiting for Charles to respond, Alice turned toward their escort and said, slowly and clearly in her classic English, "My dear man. Thank you for tonight. We do not need your assistance anymore. We have changed our plans and will dine elsewhere."

The man was calm but firm.

"But that's quite impossible, lady. I'm terribly sorry, but the boss told me to make sure you're taken care of. He was worried when you ran away. Look lady, we're here. Here it is."

Alice looked calmly at him. "But I've changed my mind."

Charles pulled her gently by the arm.

"Don't complicate things now. You're asking for trouble."

"I will not accept charity from criminals," she snapped, possessed by a boldness completely new to her.

Charles looked at her—a woman with crazy determination in her eyes. He crouched and did what he usually does when he needs time to think. He lit a cigarette.

A Winston.

Alice looked around. Across the street there were two small Italian restaurants, as cozy as the one they stood outside of. Candlelight and checkered tablecloths. Outside the restaurants a couple of bouncers were following what was happening outside Cucina Carmela with great interest. She shifted her gaze further down the street. There were restaurants along the entire block, with old fashioned signs and flickering flames from the candelabras in the windows.

And people who were standing there staring at them.

But sometimes—and especially in this story—small miracles happen when you least expect them. Across the street, just a little bit further down the block, a familiar van stood parked, a white van with *Mr. Chow's Fish* printed in large letters on the outside. Through the window, Li Ming could be seen sitting there smoking a cigarette. Frank Sinatra streamed from the open windows in a soft, moving rendition of *Autumn in New York*.

Alice crossed the street quickly and hurried toward the white fish van.

Charles stood there watching uncertainly as she ran off. He looked over at Sal's colleague who was standing beside him staring at the European lady hurrying across the street. Charles sighed. He'd had enough trouble earlier in the day. He had no intention of getting into more. Not even for Alice's sake.

The man had dropped his cigarette on the ground and turned slowly towards Charles.

"What on earth is she doing?"

"Foreigners!" replied Charles. "You know."

And without meaning to, his feet began to follow Alice towards the van.

* * *

Babylonia walked along Canal Street, turned onto Mulberry, where she was enveloped by a warm, small town feeling—an illusion, of course. But illusions were perhaps the defense mechanisms you needed to survive the reality of this city. The real reality had stayed in New Jersey, across the river in crumbling Kearny or among the monotonous little houses in Bergenfield and New Brunswick. The big rowdy city was simply bamboozling reality.

Now she just had to find Gabor and tell him that she wanted to venture out into the city. Among Dutch bartenders and strange Balkan men in wrinkled jackets. People who, incredible as it might seem, had gotten close to Alice...

But not her.

Not until now.

She wondered if she and Gabor weren't simply stuck in a rut. They were so similar, he and she. Two ordinary, cowardly middle-class kids from Europe. She needed to talk this through with him. Explain that maybe this was why she has to leave him.

But then she stopped dead in her tracks.

What she was seeing right then and there was so surreal that it must be an illusion, a figment of her imagination, brought about by her thinking about Alice. Because she couldn't possibly really be seeing her mother jump into the cargo compartment of a Chinese fish van, accompanied by a man with the most hilarious mut-tonchop sideburns.

And where had she seen him before? She closed her eyes tightly, stood still, and opened her eyes again. The van turned into a side street. And where it had been parked, a middle-aged man dressed in a black suit stood staring after it.

It couldn't have been Alice.

No, people in this city sometimes resembled each other so much, as if the city allowed people to look so odd that when push came to shove it was hard to tell them apart. At the same time, in the midst of this wonderment, she felt an additional uneasiness. A new thought that she tried to shrug off. Had she seen a vision? As if she were standing there and seeing herself in twenty years' time. As if the woman who jumped into the fish van was an apparition from the future.

Is that what would happen if she let go?

But, no, she couldn't have seen right.

She started walking again, now at a brisker pace, up toward Prince Street.

* * *

Charles held his nose and pulled out something slimy he was sitting on. "My suit," he sighed but smiled anyway, because even if he was worried about what Sal would say, he'd have to cross that bridge later. If he'd had time to think before acting, then he wouldn't be sitting in the cargo compartment of this fish van. And maybe, he thought, this *not* thinking ahead—and *not* arranging everything in perfect order—was at least a possibility.

Alice looked at Charles, the smell of fish filling her nostrils. Felt consumed by... drunk with... total madness. Was this the way it felt to lose your grip? Break down? Go mad? Everything was so incredibly crystal clear. Every contrast and edge was razor sharp.

It was as if she were studying a research animal in a cage. In the cage was the new Alice. Over-excited, filled with the present, this Alice looked around the slimy van. Impregnable. Nothing could hurt her because she was in a world that was not real. There he sat, Charles, the man she'd made love with all afternoon. He held something slimy in his hand. Fish? The van she was in was being driven by a Chinese man from Kalmar.

She found the new Alice, this mad Alice, intoxicating.

And at precisely that moment, Göran drove by in a cab. He sat in the back seat combing his hair with a Swedish steel comb. But naturally, they did not see each other, trapped as she was in the smelly fish van.

* * *

Babylonia turned left on Prince Street. A brand new apartment building stood there on the corner. Mulberry Street was changing. Next to the new building, a short Italian lady dressed in black was sweeping outside her old doorway. Next door to her building on the other side, an exclusive handbag shop had opened where just a few months earlier there had been a small newsstand.

Along Prince Street, she passed a few storefronts displaying French designer clothes, as well as a small Korean restaurant. SoHo's elegance was pressing in from one side and Chinatown from the other. The characteristic Italian everyday life that had been part of Mulberry Street for so long would soon be gone. The city would change beyond recognition and ordinary people, those who lived their lives along these streets as they'd been living them for more than half a century, would be relegated to the periphery on the outskirts of Brooklyn and Queens. Babylonia saw that this was starting already, and realized that there was nothing she could do about it. She had realized early on that reality was something that people like her mother controlled. In all large cities, overcrowded inner city slums were inevitably transformed into attractive luxury oases for people with money.

But for now the city lived on—for people like her.

She stopped at the corner of Lafayette Street, turned and looked back towards Little Italy. On the surface, the city was still welcoming. But if she didn't have enough muscle power to handle everything on her own here, no one would come to her rescue. If she wanted to stay here and grow up, have children, grow old—then she would end up way out in the boroughs, with no connection to anything except her gloomy Hungarian boyfriend, as lonely an immigrant as she. Middle-aged—six floors up with no elevator—in a life of odd jobs and barhopping, while the graying hair and the face she met in the mirror did not belong with the life she was living.

Maybe she should have grappled with becoming an adult long ago, in the town where she'd been born? But instead she'd just broken her ties from everything, packed up and moved abroad. Like an unripe fruit. Gabor had once poetically said that a fruit that doesn't ripen where it grows, never tastes as good as one that is given plenty of time to flourish before being picked.

She crossed Lafayette Street. She passed by a gallery where she'd attended an opening just a few days earlier with Gabor. Her mother might have liked that, though the art had been full of aggression and violence.

Traffic was still heavy on Broadway and she had to wait a while before she could cross the street to continue westward on Prince Street. In the window of agnès b., a pale girl with dark red lips was folding a cardigan with tiny pearl buttons. She waved as Babylonia walked by. They had met at a party once. Delphine was her name and she ran this store. Babylonia stopped and pretended to look at the window. The display was unadorned and well thought-out. A single garment. A vase of white tulips. Nothing else. Beautiful in its simplicity. It appealed to her sense of order. Maybe she could dare to enter the store. Pursue a friendship with Delphine, get a foothold, apply for a job in there.

And it was a bit like jumping off a trampoline.

To just do it...

Dive into the unknown...

She simply took hold of the door to the boutique and stepped inside.

* * *

Meanwhile, in a restaurant three floors above Canal Street, Alice looked around, alert and hungry. The place was the size of a banquet hall, full of families and groups of formal Chinese men in suits, gathered around tables covered in white starched tablecloths displaying platters of fragrant dishes. Stark fluorescent lamps illuminated the room.

She still wasn't all there. Even if the observing Alice had joined the one who was overexcited. She felt, however, that if she let the observing Alice take over, then they would leave the restaurant. *That* Alice would be afraid of the unknown, whereas excited Alice took matters in hand and beckoned to an unsympathetic waiter who turned directly to Charles. Not her. But she didn't notice.

And the dishes started arriving, one by one: egg drop soup, stir-fried bamboo shoots with mushrooms, scallops with garlic sauce, crispy duck rolled in paper-thin pancakes and small chewy spare ribs.

And while she took a cautious spoonful of savory soup, Charles told the story of how he got the apartment. It wasn't a strange or unusual story after all. It was like the majority of serendipitous events that determine most of what happens in this magical city. "You're sitting on a bar stool on an ordinary Wednesday, which turns out to be just the right bar stool—in the right joint—in this case the Triangle Cafe, but it could of course have been any other place," said Charles. And it turned out to be the perfect time to be sitting there, because sitting on the next stool is a bearded artist named Per, who happens to be from your home country. Per, in turn, inherited the apartment from a Norwegian girlfriend, Trude Andersen, a girl who had previously been dating a guy named Salvatore Genoa, who renovated bathrooms in the building on Mulberry Street in the late 1970s. And through this chain of strangers, you suddenly end up the tenant in a small drab apartment in a perfect location, that would never have been put on the market. In other words, an ordinary apartment story in New York, which, however, seems completely incomprehensible to a person who grew up with a government housing agency, where even bribes can't help arrange housing.

Between mouthfuls of the paper-thin pancakes with hoisin sauce,

Alice shook her head and decided that everything Charles said was perhaps not entirely true.

And the food was divine, so we leave Charles and Alice alone for a while, up there among all the lovely fragrances, and waiters bearing their silver trays laden with sweet-and-sour soups, shrimp dumplings, bottles of Tsingtao beer, and pots of jasmine tea, and move instead three floors down, back to the street where Gabor is walking along wheeling his bike.

He had missed Babylonia by a block and was therefore completely unaware that she was sitting and drinking strong French coffee inside a boutique with a girl named Delphine, who would soon change her life, that she would soon take a completely different path than anyone had anticipated. But we'll get back to that in a moment. For now, Gabor was blissfully unaware of these precise details. Instead, he crossed the Bowery and turned onto Catherine Street.

He passed the bar called BAR, and stopped abruptly. On the stoop to number 120 sat a man in a rumpled linen suit.

No introduction was necessary. Gabor realized that this was the father. Babylonia's father, Göran.

Gabor stood there gripping the handlebars of his bike and wondered if he should just turn and walk away. Wished he were at home in Budapest where buildings often had multiple entrances. Back entrances, delivery entrances, servants' entrances. But here in Chinatown, where the buildings were constructed for the streams of immigrants who flooded the city in the early 1900s, here he had no alternatives. The building had only one entrance.

A young couple passed by him on a moped. A kitten ran along the curb. Gabor watched as the cat stopped to sniff a few slightly rotted vegetables. He wondered if he should simply turn around and go pick up food at one of the places up by Chatham Square to avoid having to meet the man. Food was important, he thought, placing his hand almost unconsciously on his stomach. It rumbled alarmingly. The stomach was important and his was sensitive. It lived a life of its own and punished him severely if he didn't take care of it.

He was about to turn around when he realized that Göran had seen him standing there, staring. Göran stood up and waved at him now. Gabor sighed, realizing that he was stuck, grasped the handlebars again and reluctantly rolled up to the building entrance and the man leaning against it.

Gabor held out his hand. "You must be Babylonia's father."

Göran took it in his own, slightly damp, hand.

"Are you the boyfriend? I don't remember your name."

"Gabor."

"Gabor, that was it, yes."

With his most melancholy Eastern European humor Gabor replied, "Happy to hear that you at least know I exist. That was more than she remembered."

Göran looked puzzled. He unbuttoned his jacket, was sweaty as if the cool night air was a sauna.

"She?"

"Your wife."

"My wife? Alice?"

"Yes, Alice. She didn't know I existed. At all."

Göran smiled unexpectedly.

"She can be like that."

"I see."

They stood there fidgeting for a while. Moved so the lady in the shop next door could empty a pail of dirty water out into the street.

"Is she here?" Göran asked, finally. "I've come to talk things over with her."

"But," said Gabor slowly. "I mean... you really came all the way here to talk? Couldn't you have called first?"

Göran didn't respond. He just stood there, swaying and holding on to the building façade. And Gabor realized that he could let neither Alice nor Babylonia see him in that state. The man was drunk and in desperate need of coffee.

* * *

Amanda looked up as Gabor came in with a pitiful looking man dressed in an expensive but rumpled linen suit.

At Gabor's request, she poured a cup of black coffee and a club soda with ice. The man's English wasn't that good. They tried German, Dutch and then English again.

This guy, Göran, is the husband, Amanda realized. The one who had dumped her new friend Alice for a younger woman in Berlin. But what was he doing here?

She invited him to sit, poured more coffee, black as ink. Intended to give him a hard time, but he seemed so lost, drunk and so very lame in the ill-cut linen suit, which certainly had been fashionable ten years earlier. But she wasn't in the habit of punishing people and instead put her hand over his on the sticky bar counter and asked softly, "How are you doing, love?"

Pavel sat at the end of the bar, next to Melvin and Bob, and rocked back and forth on his chair. Gabor met his gaze and saw an amused chill in the Yugoslavian's eyes. A glimpse of madness he didn't want to know more about, so he turned back toward Amanda and saw Göran was now being served a large glass of water.

This will probably work out fine, he thought, without feeling too confident.

* * *

Babylonia almost danced back home after her impulsive meeting with Delphine. On Saturday, she would start working there. No longer be part of the enclave of immigrants walled off by a job related to their homeland.

She sashayed past the bar called BAR without seeing Gabor and her father Göran. And no one inside saw her walk by. No one except Bob with his nice hair, standing by the door on his way home. He said nothing. Only waved a little and wasn't sorry when she didn't wave back. He was accustomed to not being noticed despite his marcelled hair and fine lipstick.

She waltzed up the stairs of 120 Catherine Street, stopped and listened for the rooster who was dead silent at this hour of the day. A musty smell emanated from the apartment. Up on their floor, she opened all the troublesome locks and stood staring into the desolate refrigerator which, although it wasn't as empty as yesterday, still lacked proper food. Only one package of cream cheese and two Brooklyn Lagers. The pure drabness of it all struck her again. She couldn't allow herself to sink into that feeling again. Had to shape up. Retain the feeling she had when she was dancing home from her new job.

She opened a beer, took out a packet of digestives and sat on one of the uncomfortable chairs, nibbled cream cheese-covered biscuits while she pondered. And waited.

* * *

There was really nothing wrong with the man, thought Gabor, as he sat at the bar looking at Göran.

With sweeping gestures, he told a completely irrelevant anecdote from when he was a young man visiting Amsterdam in the 1970s. He was a bit boorish, maybe a little nebulous. But Gabor couldn't put his finger on what it was that didn't quite correspond to the image that Babylonia had painted of her father. And it was strange how he, Göran, no longer seemed upset. The guy was charming and chatty—so different from the other people at the bar: an elderly couple who mostly sat and stared into their glasses in silence, and that aggressive giant who just sat there and glared from the other end of the bar.

Gabor began to wonder if Göran really had come here for Alice's sake. He seemed to already have forgotten her. Like he was here as an ordinary tourist or businessman. He offered people cigarettes—and in fact, flirted with the beautiful bartender, Amanda.

Gabor sat there on his bar stool, feeling alone and superfluous, his stomach screaming. He knew that if he didn't get some food soon, that sharp pain below his diaphragm would grab hold of him again. Like a long, narrow stiletto straight into the pit of his stomach.

But Göran said he was happy to wait in the warm company of the people here. The beer was cold and good and the drab bar reminded him of some places he'd visited in the eastern parts of Berlin a long time ago.

So Gabor bid them farewell and promised to return as soon as he found Alice or Babylonia.

He went out into the street and filled his lungs with the East River breeze. The air felt fresher now. The street lay still. The Asian stores had closed. But the kitten was still there. Fearlessly rummaging among the fruits and greens under the vegetable stand.

Gabor unlocked his bike and walked back toward the brightly lit restaurants at Chatham Square.

* * *

Feeling sated and sleepy, Alice wandered by Charles's side down towards Catherine Street to pick up her bag. Felt her tension begin to fade. Now she just longed to crawl into a soft bed, wake up tomorrow and start addressing what she would do next. Perhaps dare to deal with the feeling that had sent her here from across the Atlantic.

She had phoned and booked a room at the hotel where they'd had their drinks. Thought that she needed time alone. But now she found herself wondering if she wouldn't invite Charles to join her anyway. That his hand in hers would have a calming effect in itself. This was a new feeling, this reaching out for intimacy, not always feeling compelled to fend for herself.

She passed the spot where she had stood the night before in torn stockings, without money or direction, a little drunk, paralyzed by how foreign everything seemed. Now she didn't find the city in the least bit gloomy and scary anymore. This was Babylonia's neighborhood, Alice felt welcome here, at home already, almost. Never before had she felt so enveloped by a new city. Invited to become a part of everything. Breathing deeply, she took Charles's arm.

They passed the bar called BAR and she wanted to go in and thank Amanda for taking care of her—assure her that it hadn't been her fault that Alice had become embroiled in a roulette game.

She was just about to pull open the door when she saw a familiar profile inside.

There, on a bar stool inside the bar, sat her husband.

There sat the man she'd raised a child with, the man with whom she bought a villa in Äppelviken, spent summers in Öland with, the man with whom she shared Saturday night dinners, in whose company she went for winter walks around Djurgården and Drottningholm, the man with whom she baked Christmas cookies, and with whom she routinely—about four times a month—had sex. The man who'd been having an affair with a younger woman in Berlin for an indefinite number of years, during which she had suspected—nothing.

That man was sitting there, right now, inside the bar called BAR. And he was laughing!

It was very strange.

Charles raised his eyebrows. "What is it?"

"My husband," she said simply—almost whispering.

He looked through the window pane of the door to the bar.

"My husband from Sweden is sitting there, in a linen suit, drinking."

Charles didn't think this was particularly strange. He just waited for her next move. "What do you want to do?" was all he said, calmly.

She stood still and considered what she wanted. On the one hand...! But on the other hand...! Act impulsively. Or be reasonable. Realized that he had come here to look for her and Babylonia. That it wasn't pure coincidence that he was sitting in a small bar on Catherine Street in New York's Chinatown dressed in his favorite suit, the one she knew he felt his finest in.

She turned to Charles. Felt once again that she was just floating in a tunnel where decisions were being made outside of what she really would choose for herself.

"I'll get my stuff tomorrow," she said slowly. "Let's forget the hotel for now."

"Huhu," he said simply.

"Can we go back to your place? Is he still in the building, that Sal?"

He shook his head. "I don't think so. He's a family man."

And Charles, who saw that the female bartender had caught sight of them through the pane of glass in the door—that she waved at them to come in—briskly pulled Alice away and they walked hand-in-hand back up toward Little Italy.

And through a window at the Chinese takeaway place in Chatham Square, Gabor saw them walk by. Should he call out to them? He decided that enough was enough. He wanted to go home and eat, talk with Babylonia and be left in peace.

He turned away from the window and picked up the brown bag with the fried rice and spare ribs he'd ordered.

* * *

At the same moment, Göran grudgingly accepted a Stoly from Pavel. What did this weird, burly, ugly guy want anyway? He toasted but felt uncomfortable when Pavel sat down next to him.

But Amanda, she was nice and really listened to him. He began to tell her what was really going on. He would have wanted to tell her so much more. He couldn't explain everything to Amanda. But she cocked her head and, just like most of the wonderful people who work behind drab wooden bar counters impregnated by years of alcohol and cigarette smoke, she was good at listening and offering a bit of compassion where it was most needed.

20

Later, in the small apartment on Mulberry Street, Charles leaned over his turntable, lifted the arm and flipped the record over.

"This is nice," he said. "You're going to like this. A live recording with Miles from 1969."

He turned around when he got no response.

Alice lay there on his bed, fully clothed and fast asleep, without having called Babylonia or even taken off her shoes.

He sat down beside her and caressed her hair. She didn't wake up, so he turned down Miles, turned out the lights and just sat there smoking one last evening cigarette, looking at this woman who'd appeared in his life so suddenly.

Perhaps it's enough to go with the flow and be grateful for everything as long as it lasts, he reflected.

He pulled down the blinds so that the city lights wouldn't wake her. She needed to sleep. Tomorrow, he would take her to a museum or on an excursion to one of the beaches out on Long Island.

Gently, he took off as many of her clothes as he could without waking her. Then he pulled the blanket over her, undressed and lay down beside her. Wide awake, he lay there and looked at the ceiling, thinking that he probably hadn't gone to bed this early in more than thirty years.

Outside on the street, Sal and his colleagues had gone home to their families long ago, and the super had gone in and was now lying on his back snoring beside his wife.

Further down the street, Bob and Melvin were walking arm-in-arm, supporting each other as they always did. Bob in his high heels and Melvin in his worn shoes, the black 1940s winklepickers he'd purchased at the Salvation Army.

They wouldn't sleep at Bob's place on Catherine Street tonight, but rather in Melvin's apartment at the corner of Mulberry and Spring, where Eve, the Siamese cat, waited to be fed something other than mice.

After Charles had fallen asleep, Alice woke up and lay there looking around in the dark. Wondered if she'd dreamed that she'd seen Göran. Listened to the sounds in the room that was both foreign and familiar now. The birds that moved sleepily in the cage, the water that flowed through the old pipes. The distant sound of a police siren from another part of the city.

Three days ago, she was living an uncomplicated life. Her thoughts had mostly revolved around work and everyday things such as a new spark plug for the car or a missed visit to her father at the nursing home.

Would she still have a job or a career when she got back to Sweden? Was taking off without notice so unforgivable that she would be forced into taking sick leave?

She, Alice Berglund, never called in sick.

And the night scared her as she slowly began to come to the realization that what she had done to her colleagues and others was atrocious. She was supposed to sit on Mårten's thesis committee. Had a meeting with her father's case worker at the nursing home in Vällingby. She had to go back. Enough was enough. She didn't belong here. Good lord, what had this cost her?

She sat up. Leaned against the wall. But what was she going home to? A single life in a desolate house. A career at a standstill where her colleagues would soon outpace her. Is that what she really wanted?

He snored lightly there beside her. The stranger, Charles. Who didn't care about a career back home but just slipped out of the cocoon and continued to be free. A compulsive gambler and God only knows what else. His life had no continuity, nothing she could relate to.

She stood up. Listened to the city, walked over to the window and looked out at the small concrete courtyard. The smelly finches moved quietly in the cage above her. And above that, higher still, was the sky. But the room felt confining. The walls didn't yield. There were endless possibilities outside the door. But the room itself felt like a prison.

And there on the floor was the head-hunting spear from the Philippines, a symbol that things don't mean anything if you take them out of context.

Meanwhile, in the early light of dawn across the Atlantic in a garden in the Stockholm suburb of Äppelviken, stood a solitary deer. Greedy and focused, he ate an entire bed of colorful nasturtiums outside the kitchen window where a woman had had a breakdown less than forty-eight hours ago.

21

But in the magical city it was still the middle of the night.

High above the dark courtyard where Alice stood watching the shadows, lights from millions of different kinds of lamps glittered in windows. And sound filled the air, like a concert by a huge symphony orchestra. Burglar alarms that no one bothered to report mixed with creaking beds and the sounds of people chopping celery or arguing about the rent. Or they laughed, or perhaps were too quiet while they read complicated and confusing books that they would never admit they barely understood. Maybe they snored while the theme music to *The Twilight Zone* on Channel 11 was mixed with sounds from small hungry mice who were nibbling someone's last package of cereal. Maybe five French fashion designers were partying to Marvin Gaye blasting way too loudly on a roof that was black and soft. And despite the late hour, there were undoubtedly thousands of Brooklynites on their way home riding various rattling subway trains making their way too quickly through centuries-old tunnels that felt cramped and claustrophobic if you dared to think how the entire antiquated system could fall apart at any minute.

Or maybe you were just standing with another person on a roof in Chinatown, on Catherine Street in lower Manhattan, each savoring the last drops of a Brooklyn Lager.

This particular Brooklyn Lager slipped down more easily than usual and Babylonia regretted that she hadn't bought more. A single beer made her just a little tipsy. Two beers would have made things clearer, what she now wanted to talk to Gabor about. Alcohol made your thoughts seem so sensible and her own reasoning could perhaps be more comprehensible even to herself, now that she was ready to pull herself together and explain to Gabor what she wanted and what she felt. But the beer was gone and he hadn't brought any more with him when he came up to the roof to look for her.

They had eaten the fried rice and the spare ribs up there on the roof and she imagined the greasy food would give him a stomach ache.

He put his arm around her and she leaned her head against him, breathed in his familiar scent. Maybe you were never sure you loved someone when you were still together. Maybe true love was something that you recognized only when it was too late.

She stood there with her nose against his chest and breathed, lifted her head up and looked at the city over his shoulder, saw the two World Trade Center towers down there in downtown Manhattan. They stretched toward the heavens and she thought they were impregnable and eternal. It was strange to think that they stood so tall that airplanes on their way to Newark Airport almost brushed against them.

* * *

And Göran, well, he stayed at the bar called BAR for a long time, sitting there in his white linen suit, on the border between Chinatown and the Lower East Side, staring at the ethereal Amanda as she went about closing up. He didn't quite know how he'd managed to get so drunk. He had to get back to the hotel. He'd deal with

Alice tomorrow. But she—this woman, Amanda—mesmerized him as she placed a small cup of espresso in front of him.

"You need this now, dear," she said and her tenderness almost made him cry.

"Can you phone a taxi?" he asked. "I have to get back to the hotel now."

"Taxi? Absolutely not! You're coming with us," she said firmly. "We'll show you the real New York."

She leaned over the bar and put her hand amicably over his, staring directly into him with concern in her big, green mesmerizing eyes.

"We're going to a place nearby. Come with us. We'll take care of you. You need friends like us now."

"Friends like us," echoed Pavel still sitting there with an empty beer in front of him.

Amanda locked the door. Pavel helped to drag down the gates.

Then she took Göran's hand and pressed it lightly.

"Come now. Let's go."

Göran felt as if he were floating on a wave, as if he couldn't stop what was happening, that his only choice was to accompany them, though he didn't know anything about where they were going. The only option open to him was to walk with this woman and the burly man, through dirty streets full of garbage and odors from rotting vegetables that were strewn outside closed vegetable stands. He held Amanda's hand and felt the tall man from old Eastern Europe breathing down his neck. And he had no idea where they were headed and couldn't do anything about it if he had.

But Amanda held his hand and gave Pavel a sharp look so he lowered his eyes and slowed his pace.

* * *

Babylonia sat up in bed next to her Gabor from Rózsadomb, Budapest, now asleep on his stomach, naked. She watched him silently. Didn't want to wake him. Allowed her finger to caress his shoulder where black hair grew thin as grass. Felt restless. Wide awake. Crawled cautiously out of bed without disturbing him. Paced restlessly around the apartment, but was drawn like a magnet to the window where she stood and looked over at the bar on the corner. All the lights were off and it was dark now.

The street below was deserted. Across the way, the women sat and worked at their sewing machines. What were they thinking? Did they feel the same restlessness she felt? Or had their own restlessness brought them to sewing machines in a new country?

She crawled out on the fire escape with Gabor's cigarettes in her hand. Didn't want to smoke, but needed to focus her restlessness on something.

A group of people came walking briskly down from the Bowery. Their voices echoed between the houses. And there was Delphine, astride sleek stiletto-heeled Manolo Blahniks, sandwiched between two boys, as if sent by the city to Babylonia on the fire escape above Catherine Street.

Babylonia stared and thought that nothing is a coincidence, or that maybe everything is, and she must hop on the train that was rolling past before it was too late and she missed her chance. As they passed beneath her window—before she could change her mind—she leaned over the edge of the fire escape and shouted, "Delphine. Hey. Hello."

Delphine stopped and looked up, not in the least bit surprised. She just waved a simple "Join us."

And as if someone else had taken hold of her, Babylonia, dressed and with her golden red hair in a high ponytail, found herself with Delphine and her friends headed to a place that they had a special invitation to, a new club under a ping-pong hall. "Like a speakeasy, a secret place. Everyone goes there," said Delphine.

Sure, thought Babylonia. She had left a note for Gabor, a few quick words on the back of a pizza menu. But felt that, in making this decision, just rushing out like this, there was no going back. She had stepped onto an express train toward a different life and from now on she couldn't turn around and go back. The door to life with Gabor slammed shut and locked behind her.

And Gabor, he slept on, blissfully unaware that she had defected.

22

In a brightly lit hall at the foot of the Williamsburg Bridge, two tall, athletic young men were playing ping-pong. They played silently, completely focused on the game. The venue was bare and unattractive. Aside from the sound of the ball bouncing on the table, there was only the faint whir of a ceiling fan, accompanied by the desolate hum of a vending machine.

Delphine grabbed the handle to a trapdoor. Babylonia peered through the opening in the floor and saw worn stone steps that led down to a dark room. The smell of cigar and cigarette smoke wafted up. The sound of music was intermingled with the fanint murmur of voices.

The guys followed close behind and closed the door above them.

When her eyes had adjusted to the dark, she noticed that the room was full of people who were milling around in the dimness. Argentinian music was playing from the discreetly placed speankers, and ghostlike people were smoking and drinking on couches in the dark corners of the room. Many of them from uptown, young and middle-aged, all of them dressed like extras on a film set. A couple was dancing a sensual tango and a cloud of sweet smoke rose around her.

And with a drink in hand, she suddenly finds herself right next to Amanda who, after a couple of soft tango steps, pulls her down onto a couch, puts her arm around her and whispers a soft compliment in her ear. The Dutch woman smells of booze, cigarettes, perfume and something else that is deliciously intoxicating and is simply Amanda's own personal scent. Babylonia closes her eyes and let it all happen.

And without them being aware, Göran walks past right behind the couch where his stepdaughter is sitting with Amanda.

With Pavel's arm around his back, he is on his way to try his luck at roulette. There's supposed to be a VIP room that you can only get into if you have connections. "Which I have," claims Pavel.

Göran likes the feeling of having access to something special—to something only accessible to a select few.

But the fact that, a little drunk and caught up in a sense of finally having fun, he passes two feet behind his stepdaughter Babylonia—this coincidence is naturally not important to our story.

It's just the kind of thing that happens in a big city.

* * *

Alice wakes up, once again beside the Danish man Charles, owner of a used head-hunting spear. She sits up and is suddenly certain that she's going to return home. Not yet. But soon. She stands at the window under the smelly green finches and sees the sun rise over the city, the light turning the outlines of buildings around her into a soft, fuzzy gray.

On the other side of the concrete courtyard, the light is on in a single window. Maybe there's a woman over there in a cramped little Manhattan kitchen having a nervous breakdown, with a shattered glass pitcher at her feet, howling like a banshee as she throws her husband's neckties into the dishwasher before she takes off—without bothering to lock the door behind her and with just a suitcase in her hand.

Alice closes her eyes and visualizes the desperate woman in the kitchen in Äppelviken. Had that really been her? Just a heartbeat ago?

There she stands in the silvery dawn on the other side of the Atlantic, thinking calmly that she can't possibly go back to the same life. But since there's nothing she can do about it right now—she'll do something about it another day.

In the cage above her, the finches have begun chirping, welcoming the new morning. Charles moves next to her, opens his eyes, looks at her, and pulls her down to him, cupping her right breast in his hand.

* * *

Meanwhile, in tourist-Chinatown, two Chinese boys are running down Mott Street. They are carrying something big and unwieldy between them in a brown paper bag. No one pays any attention to them, except the opera singer who watches them lasciviously from a cafe across the street. This does not bode well, he shudders delightfully, with the same excited feeling that usually spreads across his stomach at the end of the second act. Not good at all.

And what happens next, well, that's a whole 'nother story.

* * * * *

ABOUT THE AUTHOR

Raised in tranquil Stockholm, Ingrid Rudefors always dreamt of the big city. Immediately after finishing high school, she packed her bags and left for New York.

From 1977 to 1993, she lived in the then-quite-derelict East Village, frequenting the downtown club scene. This period provided inspiration for the characters, locations and situations in this novel.

Rudefors has also written and directed several award-winning short films, among them the 1990s cult-short *A Woman's Point Of View During Sex*. She has written three feature-length screenplays with support from the Swedish Film Institute and has worked for twenty years in the film industry in New York and Stockholm, serving for eight years as the Film Commissioner of Stockholm.

She returned to Stockholm in 1993 to raise her daughter, but is now back in New York and lives with her husband on the Lower East Side, within walking distance from the Chinatown of this novel.

* * *

For more information about the author or to order copies of this book, visit www.ingridrudefors.com.

Meanwhile on a Roof in Chinatown is the first publication of Triangle Ranch Worldwide, an imprint of Triangle Ranch Communications (www.triangleranch.com) dedicated to the translation and publication of fiction by Swedish writers.

ACKNOWLEDGEMENTS

The author would like to mention those who assisted in the original Swedish version of the novel: Erik Grundström, Ann-Marie Tung Hermelin and Hedda Krausz Sjögren.

She also wishes to thank Odella Schattin for her dedication to the production of a faithful translation, a special thank you to Lori Behron for being a great editor for this edition, and also a very warm thank you to Johan Vipper for creating the cover.

And then, most of all, very special recognition is due to the backers of the Kickstarter campaign that financed the translation of this novel. Each one of you, including the anonymous donors, have helped open the doors of *Chinatown* to a much wider readership:

Martin Abrahams, Matthias van Arkel, Lena Arnström-Denaive, Staffan Aspegren, Dorothea Axelson

Beth B., Christina von Bergen, Anna Bergström, Lori Berhon, Rodrigo Bernardo, Michael Blair, Delphine Blue, Be Bop, Johan Brisinger, Robert & Robin Brown, Susan Brown Douglas, Chris Buck, Adrian Burt

Holger Carlsson, Patrick el-Cheikh, Shumaï Chou

Kristofer Dan-Bergman, Jerry Day, Rhel ná DecVandé, L. Elliott Donnelley

Erika Edman, Johan Edström, April Ekholm, Boris Enquist, Tova Epstein

Marti Fischer, Jessica Forsbenrg, Mikael Forsberg, Kelley Forsyth, Jennifer Fox

Gelwan the Inimitable, Lisa Giordano, Garnet Girl, Gittan Goding, Bob Gosse, Erik Grundström, Nicole Guillemet, Andreas Gustafsson, C. Guttman

Michael & Eva-Jo Hancock, Hal Hartley, Sue Hayes, Cecile & Howard Herskovitz, M. Herskovitz, Steven Herskovitz, Peter Hogan, Sigmund Elias Holm, Mark & Maria Holter, Anne Hubbell

Adam Isidore

Bethany Jacobson, KJ Jennings, Ingrid E. Johnson, Catherine Johnson

Leilani V. Kapili, Caroline Kaplan, Anna Knutsson, Truls Kontny, Irena Kovarova, Marie Lagerkvist

Christina Larsson, Maria Larsson, Ronnie Levine, Suzanne Levy, Tess Lindberg, Sara Lüdtke, Åke Lundström

Ingela Magner, Ulrika Malmgren, Sophia Massot, Anna Melinder, Cynthia Millman, Rickard Molin, Erica Motley

New York Inspiration

Lisa Ohlin, Miyoko Oshima, Klara Östlund

Lisa Del Papa, Åsa Pape, Misha Pavel, Lars Pettersson, Eve Pomerance, Judy Pritchett

Cornelia Ravenal, Joachim von Rost, Gun Rudefors, Håkan Rudefors, Lars Rudefors, Susann Billberg Rydholm

Eva Sandström, Margaret Savage, Brandi Savitt, Wendy Sax, Sandy Seltzer, Sharmala Sharvanandan, Adriana Shaw, Ryuhei Shindo, Simona, Elin Sleipnes, Mikael Sodersten, Jonas Söderström, Päivi Söderström, Håkan Soold, Mark Strom, Mikael Svensson & Helena Danielsson, Gabor Szitanyi

Alon Tal, Lisen Tamm, Louis Tancredi, Billy Taylor, Berit Tilly, Linus Tunström

Karol Vieker, Johan Vipper, Sarah Vogel

Rachel Watanabe-Batton, Liv Watson, Marleen van der Wende, Travis White, Daniel Wilson, Ingrid Wirén